Resa's wild dance went on until she was out of breath and giggling. She stood panting several feet away from Boone, her cheeks and forehead flushing under their strain, a crazy kid's grin on her face. Then she rushed past him again. As she did, he grabbed her hand and, laughing at her laughter, drew her to him. He kissed her eyes. He kissed her hands, making her tremble like the aspen leaves above their heads.

When Boone drew Resa to the meadow grass, a tangle of emotions knotted in her breast for she was alone with this man, a man who killed, a man who gambled, but—she was certain—a man who loved.

FRONTIER DYNASTY

BY ELIZABETH I. RISEDEN

ZEBRA BOOKS
KENSINGTON PUBLISHING CORP.

ZEBRA BOOKS

are published by

KENSINGTON PUBLISHING CORP.
475 Park Avenue South
New York, N.Y. 10016

Printed in the United States of America

Part One

Chapter One

The hot July wind moaned off Raton Pass. The wind slammed the door of Wootton's Station, but not before it had covered the parched room with dust. The half-breed cook swore and moved to cover the dough rising in wooden troughs. Too late. The dough was grit-sprinkled. He shrugged and went back to peeling potatoes.

Dust devils, one clockwise, one counter-clockwise seethed in the meadow below, married themselves in fury, and tore through the truck garden, whipping the corn tassles. Chickens were pushed along helter skelter, bumping into one another as they flopped toward the blacksmith shop.

The dust devil split in two. One blew itself out against the canyon walls. The other coursed through the empty meadow where wagon trains sometimes rested, then picked up some straw and a shred of newspaper with "Santa Fe, July 4, 1867." The wind slammed across the meadow, bashed the canyon wall, and dropped its load in the creek that tumbled beneath the rocks.

Three miles below the station, high on the hills above a place called The Narrow, the wind tore at the scrub oaks and the buffalo grass. Three horses, tethered out of sight of the trail below, swished off flies and pawed the ground.

The wind was escaping south to Mexico. It was a hell of a time to wait. Three men, who owned the horses, were broiling in the noonday heat. One, a boy, had chewed up the ground in front of him playing mumblety peg. His hat brim pulled down over his eyes, he cast his knife again and again into the dry soil, oblivious that the shade of the oak tree under which he had been sitting had pulled back from him. It didn't matter. The shade only made the heat denser, more compact. Between thrusts, he mopped his blond curls away from his blue eyes, poking them under his sweaty hat band. His face and hands were filthy.

The other two men sat to the backside of the tree, facing the wind, where they could watch up the canyon. One was a giant in a buckskin jerkin and high beaded moccasins, with an angry scar that twisted from under the jerkin to the hair on his forehead; the other man was splotched like a pinto, with large patches of brown skin alternated with white above his graying beard, on his worn hands, blurring his features. Between them sat a half-empty whiskey jug.

The giant, chewing a cheroot, stood. He stretched, then walked a few paces away. He peed. After buttoning up, he shaded his eyes and stared up the canyon.

"Pack train's late. What you make of it, Wooly?"

"Maybe they gotta take it easy . . . heat." The mottled man stroked his beard. He took a slug from the jug and handed it to the other man. "Hell, when I worked there something was always busting at the smelter.

11

Who knows, Mike." He belched, then leaned back against the tree.

"I want this done with. By fall, I want to be in Oregon."

"Hah! The day you ride outa here will be the day I'm an angel. You'll never settle into a ranch and you know it."

The boy stuck the knife in the ground near his boot. "All I want is to get back to Loma Parda, get me one've them fandango girls, and stay drunk for a year, pirooting around." He threw the knife again.

"Stop it, Badger. You're getting on my nerves." Mike stood over him and pushed the jug at him.

Badger took a long swallow. His eyes were red. "What I wouldn't give for a drink of cold water. Hell! If Garcia don't come back soon, we'll be too drunk to ride."

"He'll be here when the train gets here. I figure he's following it. Least that's what he's paid for."

"I don't like him," said Wooly. "He thinks he's better than everybody. He won't drink. Doesn't talk much. Then talks fancy."

"He's the best gun I've ever known," Mike said. "He's okay."

"Don't like him anyway. Comes time, you'll see who's good," Wooly said to

Badger. "Why, in '64, Mike and I rode with six others out of Santa Fe. Hit a mule train outa Vegas, was . . ."

"Looky here," Mike motioned Wooly to shut up. "Ain't that the wagon belongs to them McCutcheon folks ate with us at Wootton's this morning?"

"Them hoity-toity folks with the gal in the titty-tight dress? The woman with the pearls? When we met them butter wouldn't melt in her fancy-pants mouth," Wooly spat.

"Yeah. Prideful hag."

"Her man's a fool more ways than one. Out here by hisself." Wooly dragged on the jug, then passed it to Mike.

"Heard him tell the blacksmith they threw a tire coming down the pass. Wanted to let his missus rest before they catch up to their party."

"Bet there's more than them pearls," Wooly smiled at Mike.

"Hell, why not? Beats waiting on Garcia."

"You're not gonna kill them?" said Badger.

"Hell, no. Just get the jewelry. What can they do? They've got a fool, a boy, and two women—one just a baby. They won't try anything."

"We oughta wait for the gold."

"What I say, you do," Mike barked, then walked to his horse; the others followed. "Hell, we'll be back in half an hour."

"It's a hell of a chance for no reward."

"Shut up, Badger. Anything beats sitting in this heat." They rode down the mountain, staying in the trees, angling their descent to come out just to the side of the wagon, at the south end of the meadow before the narrows.

The McCutcheons' covered wagon, pulled by four mules, rolled across the meadow. Its canvas top was stained with red dust, brown dirt, and yellow clay—remainders of the soil they'd been through. Water barrels were lashed to the sides. Tar, for maintaining the wheels, swung in a bucket below the right barrel.

Maud rode on the front seat. Her sunbonnet covered her face, but her skin was too fair for the frontier, and was now wrinkled by months of sun to dry parchment. McCutcheon, rail-thin, his once-fine suit coat hanging on his shoulders, glanced at her.

In the back Resa rode on a pile of folded sougans. Her red-checked calico, faded to pink, caught the perspiration that ran down

the back of her neck. She held her bisque-
headed doll, Elspeth, and peeked out between her parents.

Peter rode in the rear of the crowded
wagon on some boxes of store goods. His
dark hair, like McCutcheon's, was matted
with sweat. He held a Remington and
rubbed its stock.

"Trail's almost beaten us, but we'll be
there soon," McCutcheon said.

"This is a desert full of ruffians!" Maud
complained. "It's common. We're raising
our children common. It's terrible for a
McCutcheon woman to live like this, and
for Resa to be growing up this way." She
turned to the children. "We're the cream in
this world, children. Don't ever forget it."
Her voice was shrill.

"I don't see how we're different from
anybody else," said Peter.

"The differences pretty much died with
the emancipation, with the end of the
plantation," said McCutcheon.

"We're *not* like everyone else. The new
ranch will set us apart. We'll have a fine
house, with servants." Maud's melodious
Georgia accent played across the meadow.
"Quality. You children must train your eye
for quality."

The three rough men clattered out of the

trees to the side of the wagon. One of the McCutcheon mules honked as Mike rode up in front and grabbed its harness. McCutcheon pulled back on the reins.

"Hide!" Maud hissed at the children. Resa dropped her doll.

Wooly and Badger, pistols drawn, backed Mike up. He trained a Henry rifle on McCutcheon.

"We admired your pearls so much, we thought we'd like them," said Mike. "Hand them over. Any other jewelry you have, too."

Maud climbed into the back of the wagon. She was pale, trembling.

"Be still," she whispered. Her hands shook as they searched for an intricately carved teak box with held several bracelets, a brooch of amythysts and gold, and her favorite piece—a necklace of rubies and diamonds set with filigree on a gold chain. She climbed back to the seat.

"Give them over," Mike said. "We don't want no trouble." He reached out his hand and took the box.

"These are my heritage," Maud said through clenched teeth. "White trash scum." Resa had never heard such rage in her mother's voice.

"You old bitch," Wooly said.

The gang turned their horses and rode away in front of the mules back the way they came, seeking cover in the sparse growth.

The mules started forward. Up front, Maud and McCutcheon sat like stones.

Peter jumped out the back of the wagon. As the men passed, he aimed his rifle and fired.

"Peter!" Resa cried. She ran to the back of the wagon. She heard McCutcheon cock his .38. Wooly was lying in the grass. His horse stood near him. The other two men took cover in the trees. Peter fired again.

Maud grabbed the reins and put on the brake. McCutcheon clambered down from his seat and scrambled beneath the wagon. He fired. Badger and Mike fired back. With a cry, Peter fell. Resa screamed.

Maud dropped the reins and climbed down. She ran toward her son. The mules brayed and jumped in their traces. They dragged the wagon forward, leaving McCutcheon exposed.

"Get down!" McCutcheon yelled to his wife. Heedless, Maud ran on. Two more shots rang out. She crumpled near Peter's body. Resa screamed and covered her eyes.

For a moment there was silence. Then there were two more shots. McCutcheon moaned. From the floor of the wagon where

17

Resa had fallen, she heard him cry out again. Then all was still.

She was certain they must be dead. All dead. Her mother. Her father. Her brother. All dead. The hot wind smothered her sobs as she searched mechanically through their supplies until she found their Green River knife. She grasped it tightly in her hand. The wind sobbed as she tunneled under the pile of sougans. The air seemed thin. She barely breathed.

Dead. Her family was dead. Somewhere near the wagon, in the howling wind, the men waited.

Resa told herself to keep still. If she could stay still, maybe someone would come to see what was wrong. She might have a chance.

The wagon shook as somebody climbed into it.

"Let's have a look. There's bound to be more." His voice was deep.

Again the wagon shook. They were throwing everything out, heaving boxes. With each crash, each exclamation, they came closer to Resa's warren. She shrank further in on herself.

"It's a poor haul."

"Here's blankets."

A flash of light blinded her momentarily. A draft swooped around her shoulders. Resa

18

jumped to her feet and started flailing blindly with the knife at the figure who tossed the blankets aside. She was slashing, screaming, flailing at air, when a heavy blow knocked her back to the wagon floor. The knife skittered out of her hand, landing just out of her reach in front of a pair of moccasins with blue lightning beaded on the sides.

A hand reached out and dragged her to her feet.

"Why, you little pole cat." Mike loomed over her. He smelled like the dead buffalo they'd passed along the Arkansas. His greasy buckskin jerkin was open at his throat. His scar, reddened with excitement, attracted Resa's stare. She was fascinated by its hideous track. He shook her by the shoulders until she felt her head would fly off.

"Sonofabitch. I thought she ran off." Badger stood up and stared at her. Fresh blood splotched the front of his shirt.

"Get on with the sorting, Badger. I'll take care've this little lady."

"Didn't know you was interested in babies."

"I'll get her out've the way. Garcia'll be back any time."

"C'mon little lady. You'n me's taking a

19

walk." Mike pushed Resa in front of him toward a rock outcropping that spit out from a pine grove. She hit at him as he pushed her. She saw her father's body, slumped forward in the buffalo grass. Mike caught her hand, she clawed at him. They passed the edge of the clearing where Peter lay face up, with his arm twisted unnaturally behind him. His sightless eyes stared to heaven. She wished she could close them.

"My ma!" she shrieked.

"Dead. She was right stupid, your old lady. Wearing them trinkets. If she'd've been mine, I'd've seen her horsewhipped fore I let her parade them jewels."

Resa leapt at him and pounded at his chest. She dug her nails into his arms and kicked at his moccasined feet. Blind with rage, she flailed at him until he put out his huge hands and captured both of hers.

"Somebody should've told your ma that pride goeth before a fall. Should've told your brother that, too." He dragged Resa along as she kicked and squealed until he hoisted her on his shoulder and carried her the last few feet to the trees. As he lifted her up, a rosary fell out of her pocket.

"That'll make a swell trade for them Santa Fe papists." Mike threw her like a sack of rags to the ground.

He was on her, then, holding her hands pinned with one hand while, with the other, he drew up her skirts. In haste, he tried to pull down her pantaloons and ended ripping them from between her crossed legs. She screamed; screamed until he cuffed her semi-senseless. A hot fog drifted over her, mingling with the pain that shot through her as he pried open her legs like a rail splitter driving a wedge; he thrust into her again and again, scourging her, grunting like the pigs she'd seen coupling—much to her mother's horror—in Georgia.

Later, she was to know other women who had been raped. They would tell her they couldn't remember much about it. Resa would not be so lucky. She never forgot it, and the vivid details—Mike's body, his smell, the sky and pines whirling around her, the jagged stone that pierced the small of her back where her chemise ended, the unmentionable pain and hurt of it—stayed as real to her as any reality she knew.

At last, Mike stopped hunching and grunting. She lay, momentarily, as though dead while he got up, hitched up his pants. At the wagon, she heard laughter.

"C'mon, Mike," Badger called. "Let's go."

Instantly she was on her feet, running.

She leaped over a deadfall. A shot rang out. She knew he'd shot at her and missed.

"Sonofabitch!" He was right behind her.

Out of the corner of her eye, she glimpsed a black and white pinto and rider.

"Argh." She turned. Mike fell back as the handle of an Arkansas toothpick pushed through his throat. Blood splashed onto his jerkin. He was still. Resa sank to the ground where she had been standing. Sobs racked her shoulders. She knew she should run onward, hide, protect herself. Yet she could no more move than fly.

She looked over her shoulder. Badger was stooped over Mike listening for a heart beat. He took Mike's pistol and holster. "Christ! You killed him."

"Yes."

The voice came from in front of her. She looked up, her body gathering itself to run again.

"What a pig. She's just a baby." The voice belonged to the man called Boone Garcia. He was tall and wore buckskins. His black hair curled beneath his black hat. His dark eyes were set deep in a tanned, serious face. For the first time Resa looked down at herself. Her calico was ripped up the front and torn down the back of the skirt. Her petticoat was ripped, too. Something warm oozed onto it. She felt shame.

The man who had killed Mike stood a couple of yards away from her. Like a man gentling a skittish colt, he talked to her.

"Now don't go bolting on me," he said as he walked toward her. "I won't hurt you." Over his shoulder he said, "Unhitch the mules, Badger. Turn two loose; we can use two at the cache. Get Wooly's horse, too. Hurry, the train's only an hour away. What a damnfool trick. I hired on to get gold, not to rob families. Now we've gotta run. Leave the gold behind."

"You bringing her?"

"Can't see any choice."

"Mike said to kill her."

"She comes. But she needs food and clothes first."

"We've got to kill her."

"Don't make me draw to prove my point," Garcia said evenly.

Badger shrugged his shoulders and walked to where Wooly's horse was standing. He led the horse toward the wagon.

Garcia took Resa by the arm, and steered her toward the wagon. He hunted for food in the piles on the ground.

"What's your name, girl?"

"Resa."

"How old are you?"

23

"I'll be fourteen next week."

He shoved some jerky at her. "C'mon, let's get you some clothes. You ride?"

"Back home, in Georgia, I rode in meets."

"Can you stick to a horse in this country?"

"Sure."

"Good. You'll have Mike's. You've got to mind him; he's skittish near water . . . wants to dump anybody when he gets near a stream."

She was numb. Too numb to think why Boone Garcia had saved her life. Too numb to question the clothes he slapped in the saddlebags for her. They were Peter's clothes and too big for her. She was too numb to taste the jerky, deadened to the bodies strewn about the campsite, anesthetized against the sight of Peter twisted against the earth. She sat on the ground like a statue. Garcia had to prod her to put on the clothes he tossed to her. She didn't even think of going behind the wagon to change. Nor did she question it when he dragged the bodies of her pa and ma and Peter and Wooly into the wagon and set the whole thing ablaze.

"I haven't time nor stomach for Christian burials," he said, as he set the wagon on fire. "Besides, they'll think you were burned in it, too. Can't have somebody tracking after us when it's easy to make it look like Indians."

The shadows told her it was about three o'clock when she, Garcia, and Badger rode out, trailing two mules and Wooly's horse. She left behind her childhood and her virginity, the threads that bound her existence together.

Chapter Two

Resa rode in front of Garcia, with Badger bringing up the rear. She slouched in the saddle and she prayed, mumbling the rosary under her breath.

"That prayin' gives me the willies," Badger complained to Garcia.

"Let her have it," said Garcia. "It's not doing any harm."

Badger muttered a curse and sang:

You're a beauty, Molly Brown,
With your hair ahangin' down.
You're a beauty, Molly Brown,
And when we get to town
I'll buy you a new gown
With cloth as soft as down.
You're a beauty, Molly Brown,
And I love you.

"That'll attract every Indian for miles," Garcia said.

"Just drowning our her prayin'," answered Badger as he started another chorus—more quietly.

"It's as good a funeral song for Wooly and Mike as any."

"Wooly was a snake. Mike was all right, though. You sure made a miserable trade. Mike for her."

"What were you doing in Las Vegas jail, anyhow? How'd Mike come to bail you out?" Garcia asked.

"Mike needed a replacement. Hell, I wasn't doing anything when they hauled me in. Maxwell's got so many cattle, what'd he care if I took a few?"

"Pickings have been better with this," said Garcia. He turned to Resa and said, "Missy, if you must pray, keep it down, will you?"

Resa turned to look at him defiantly. She straightened her slumped shoulders.

"I have nothing against prayer. Just against noise," Garcia assured her.

They started down toward the prairie. Mike's sorrel stumbled, then snorted. Resa's hands grabbed for the horn, but she rode, otherwise, as though in a dream.

"Mr. Garcia, can we stop a minute? I, I need . . ."

"Sure. Just don't be long. Give me the reins."

He watched her as she dismounted and handed him the reins. As she walked toward some brush, she teetered on her boots.

"She must be sore as hell," said Badger as he watched her. "What a mess. Real pitiful."

"Look again, Badger. With some care and feeding and some milk baths for her skin, she'll be mighty pretty one day soon."

"Yeah. Pretty and useful. Maybe you knew what you was doing, killing Mike for her. Why don't you let me try her out and see?"

"No."

"I'd pay."

"With what?"

"When we get to the cache, I mean. I've earned my cut. Far as that goes, I've earned Mike's and Wooly's too. They being so dear to me and all."

Garcia laughed. "Greedy, aren't you? You'd better leave after the split."

Resa walked up to them and mounted. They continued to ride in silence except for her mumbled prayers.

All around them stretched the prairie. The mountains behind them cast long shadows out onto the plains. Rolling grassland spilled off toward Las Vegas, while two or three miles away Boone saw the lone patch of trees that signaled the South Fork, their stop for the night. It was a creek that had no North Fork, having been named by some lost soul long ago. Two more days and they'd be at the cache.

They picked up their pace. Boone rode up beside Resa. "In case there's any doubt in your mind, Badger would just as soon jump you as look at you. So I advise you to make yourself small. Speak when spoken to. Make yourself useful. Above all, shut up."

"Killers!" she spat.

"And don't make cow-eyes at him."

She lifted her scrawny chin and spurred her horse ahead of his.

Their campsite lay above the creek's banks. The water, no more than a sluggish trickle in the late July heat, smelled stagnant. On the site were remnants of several fires. Some straggly cottonwoods shaded them. The brush stood high along the banks, its long roots straining toward the creek.

Every bone in Resa's body seemed made of putty. She slid off the sorrel, her head throbbing, her bones shaking. She undid the girth and lifted the saddle to the ground. The weight of the saddle almost knocked her over as she pulled it off, but she didn't let it throw her.

She leaned momentarily against the horse's shoulder, steadying herself. If she could have, she would have melted her soreness into that sweaty shoulder. She wished she could disappear into the animal and run like the wind out onto the plains.

Garcia unpacked, watered the pack animals, and hobbled them. He tethered the other horses to drink. Grabbing the reins of the sorrel high near the bit, he led the water-bucker downstream. Resa picked up the horse brush he tossed her. One at a time she brushed the horses, gentling them as they tried to walk away from her.

Soon Badger had a fire started. From a pack he got out a blackened coffee pot and coffee.

"Here. Fill this pot," Badger ordered Resa.

Resa could feel Badger's eyes on her as her legs carried her down the bank. She walked up the creek a little way. Every step brought the pain between her legs searing into her brain. Her back, where the stone had gouged it, felt raw and saddle-bruised. It was so long since she had ridden, her whole body was a mass of undefined aches.

She bent over and filled the pot. As she started back up the bank, her foot caught a sage root and she went sprawling. Water splashed her pants and shirt.

"Ain't she the graceful one," Badger mocked. "Here, fine lady, let me help you up."

"No!" Resa bounded to her feet, grabbing the pot as she rose, and started down the bank again. Badger stared from the edge down at her. "Just trying to help a lady in distress."

She got the water back to the fire and put the pot down near Badger.

"What we eating?" Garcia asked.

"Got some vegetables from the wagon.

Thought I'd try a stew. When your prize's through with the coffee, she can fill the Dutch oven, and cut up these taters and carrots. Looks like you've got a real winner there, Boone. She can't even get up a bank without tripping over her feet."

"Let the girl rest. I'll cut the vegetables," Garcia said.

Resa was so tired she would gladly have slept a year, but she knew she must not, so she walked where the horses were grazing and sat watching them. Numb.

"Resa, come get the dishes out, will you?" Boone called. As she walked toward the men, all she could think was how she hated them, how she'd like to screw herself down into the ground and disappear.

She gagged the gray stew down, thinking how her mother's would have tasted. Her eyes watered with the thought and, for the first time since they left camp, she remembered why she was here. She looked down at the dusty, mud-streaked flannel of Peter's shirt and shivered. She hated the coffee they gave her, but she forced herself to drink it. She remembered the tea her family drank. Its fragrance was her family. The others on the train had ridiculed them as tea drinkers, yet were quick enough to borrow it when anybody was ill.

Out there under the sunset to the south, the wagon train would be camped for the night. She wondered idly if they'd sent someone back by now, if someone was looking for her. She saw the faces of her friends—Clementine and Jimmy Price from the wagon in front of them, Molly and Karen Southerland from Tennessee, who talked funny and played odd games she hadn't heard of before. She heard Mr. Southerland's harmonica playing "Turkey in the Straw." Then she thought of the blazing wagon. She knew no one would come to find her.

She stood and gathered the dishes into the Dutch oven. In the last light, she took them down to the creek and washed them. Her child's hands made a game of washing, sloshing the utensils up and down. The cold water on her fingers hurt her to life. She rubbed the sore on her back.

"Resa, you trust me?"

Boone came up behind her so quietly, and she was so lost in thought that she jumped as if sprayed by a skunk.

"Whoa," he reached out and patted her shoulder. She shrank from his touch. "Don't be afraid. I noticed you rubbing your back, let me see it."

"No."

"Come back up. I've something'll make it feel better."

In the dying light she took the dishes. He filled the Dutch oven again. When they got to the fire, he set the oven in the coals. She put the dishes on a canvas near Badger. He was whittling—hacking up a cottonwood stick with no particular design. Garcia rifled through one of the packs.

"Go check on the stock," said Garcia. "Don't come back 'til I call you."

"You gonna sample Miss Priss?" Badger rose.

"Move . . . get."

While Badger walked out to the animals, Boone balanced a jar on a rock by the fire. He took a shirt from his bedroll. It was reasonably clean.

"Let me see your back. This'll make it feel better."

"No," Resa glared at him.

"I'm not going to hurt you. Hell, I'd do the same for one've the horses. A little sponging won't hurt you. You're almost as dirty as Badger."

A war raged within the battered girl. Although her back burned with pain, she was loathe to let the bandit help her. Finally, she turned her face to the fire and pulled out the tail of Peter's shirt. She held it tightly across her chest, while Boone examined her back.

"No wonder you've favoring it. It's a deep gash." He dipped his shirt tail in the warm water and cleaned the wound. She sucked in her breath, determined not to say anything about the pain. Once the stinging was over, though, she was comforted by the warm water as he washed her back in circles. He took the dry sleeves of the shirt and dried her back. Then he reached for some evil-looking black substance in the jar.

"It's ointment for the horses. Can't hurt you." He put some on his fingers and applied it to the cut. It stung terribly and she let the shirt drop. Resa bit her fingers to keep from crying out.

He stood. "I'm going out to Badger. Now finish the job. And don't try to run off. It's a lot of lonely miles to anywhere. Comanches. Starvation. If Badger or anything gives you trouble tonight, holler. I'll be right here."

As she washed herself, she imagined the men's eyes ogling her from the darkness. Yet the warm water soothed her. She washed her arms and hands; her face, her neck. She reached under the shirt and pulled up her pants' legs. The water was like a benediction. Taking the dry sleeves of Boone's shirt, she dried herself. Then she got up, smoothing her clothes, and put the wet shirt on a sage.

Out in the darkness she heard voices talking quietly.

She unrolled her bedroll, the last of the warmth of the water still on her. She climbed in between the evil-smelling blankets.

"I'm turning in," said Badger, stretching elaborately as they walked back to the fire.

"Fine. I'll take first watch. Just one thing. You touch that girl and I'll kill you."

"Sure. But it's been a long time since Santa Fe."

"Better a long time than never," said Garcia. He picked up his rifle and walked out of the light.

Resa awakened at dawn to the sound of Badger's coughing. For a while she lay under her blankets, which smelled as Mike had smelled, wishing her sleep had never ended. In the night she had screamed from a nightmare. She was reliving the deaths of her parents. In her dream they were being eaten by wolves. The wolves attacked her, too. Resa could feel their fangs breaking her skin, cracking her bones, which were bright red glass. Only a wolf on a black and white pinto had attacked the other wolves before the glass in her center was shattered. In the night she was pushed to one side, gently. Rocked awake by Boone.

"Shut her up, or shoot her," Badger mumbled.

Boone held her for awhile. He smelled like hay.

Boone, noticing her moving in the blankets, brought her some coffee. When she lifted herself up on an elbow to drink it, all the pains of the previous day hit her. She moaned.

"Here," he said. "This'll make you feel better. When you've had it, take this and do something with your hair. Can't have it gathering knots 'til it's gotta be chopped." He pushed a comb in her face. She wanted to spit at him.

After breakfast—johnnycake and bacon—they mounted up. Badger rode on one side of her, Boone on the other. Badger was singing. His curls poked out beneath his hat. Resa was fascinated by their dirty whiteness, curled against his equally dirty face.

They were pushing hard, the smell of booty luring the men like horses drawn to water after a twenty mile desert. Skirting the trails, they were forced into the foothills of the Sangre de Cristos, where they spent themselves and their horses going up and down. Sometimes, when they glimpsed the plains to the east, Resa could see antelope. She imagined praire dog towns; she entertained herself by thinking of games she and the wagon train children had played after their chores were finished. Yet with those memories came sadness. Each daisy chain of memories of happy times was followed by memories of the massacre followed by prayers for her family, prayers for the deaths of her captors. To avoid crying, she'd forced herself to stare at the world around her, memorizing each pine needle, hearing each hoof fall, straining her ears for bird calls, trying to identify which calls belonged to which birds.

That night they camped cold on the edge of the plains, Garcia fearing Comanches. Her nightmares returned. Again she felt Boone's arms holding her, only this time she didn't scream. She cried soundless tears. She cried until she was utterly drained, biting the ends of her pigtails, while his arms cradled her until she fell asleep. She awakened curled next to him with his arm flung out across her chest. Shame lit her cheeks. She shoved his arm away.

That day it rained. It rained as though God's tears were answering hers of the night. Lightning and thunder surrounded them, spooking the horses, giving her little time to think of anything except managing the skittish sorrel. Yet she took satisfaction in her soggy misery. The others were as miserable as she.

"We gotta get outa this," said Boone. "There's a cave a mile ahead if I remember right."

"Shit! I vote we go on."

"The girl looks flushed. We should get to the cave and forget the cabin until tomorrow."

"Hell, you said it wasn't far," Badger whined.

"You don't know enough to get in out of the rain."

Badger swore under his breath.

The cave was a dung-smelling niche, just about large enough for the three of them to lie flat, situated on a ledge high above the valley floor. They tethered their horses in the trees below the ledge. Resa scratched her hands against the jagged shale as she climbed to it.

At the back of the malodorous hole was an ancient fire pit. Below, Badger scrounged some half-wet wood, sent grumbling to his task because Boone couldn't leave him alone with Resa. Soon a smoky, choking fire was sputtering to feeble life. They coughed and cursed the smoke, as the men nonchalantly removed their clothes—stringing them along a blackened ledge on one side of the walls to dry. They wrapped themselves in blankets from the bedrolls.

"You gonna sit there in those soaked things?" Badger asked.

Resa sat shivering, her back to them, away from the fire, staring into the sheeting rain.

"You'll have to get out of your clothes or you'll catch your death," said Boone.

"No."

He reached over her shoulder from behind and drew her face around near his.

"I didn't save you just so you'd die of pneumonia. Now, take off those things. Wrap up in a blanket."

"C'mon, Resa, give us a treat. It's not like you're a virgin," Badger taunted.

"Shut up," Garcia glared at his partner.

"Don't look," Resa said quietly, terrified that they would.

"Course not. You've nothing to look at," Badger growled, and rubbed his arms. But his eyes were lit by a hungry glow.

Resa finally gave in and got out of her clothes, using the blanket as a screen, while Badger cheered her on. Under the blanket, her cheeks were flaming. She stayed there long enough to feel the fire in them die before she got up, and, holding the blanket with one hand, draped her clothes on the ledge.

"Make us some coffee," Badger said.

"How's she gonna do that with one hand?" said Garcia. "I'll make the coffee."

Resa noticed a knife on the ledge. She reached for it and hid it under the blanket before she went closer to the men. *I'll kill the first person who touches me.* She squatted by the fire, tucking the scratchy, horse-smelling blanket around herself, resting the knife next to her leg. The shadows on the jagged cave walls flickered spookily.

Outside, the storm raged. Night drew on. They gnawed on soggy food and drank canteen water. Soon the men dozed. Resa lay petrified; the knife at her side was cold. *I failed with a knife before. This time I can't.* Finally she fell into an exhausted, fitful sleep.

She had no idea what time it was, but the fire was out. She was wide awake. Turning her head, she saw that there were stars outside. The wind was blowing. It sighed through the piñons and junipers. It was too quiet. Something made a shiver up her back. Her hand slid slowly down, grasping

41

the knife handle. Something moved. Suddenly, a hand slid across her mouth. Another hand fumbled under the blanket. She tried to scream, but there was no sound.

Reflexively, she brought the hand with the knife up, turning simultaneously toward where her instinct told her the body was—behind her and to her left. She rolled over and slashed—aiming for the belly. She felt it connect and sink in.

"Jesus! She stuck me!"

The cave came alive with movement.

Resa was on her feet. She tripped over someone as she headed out of the cave.

"Bitch! Wildcat!" Badger's voice shrilled.

She was barefoot and naked except for the blanket. The rocks tore at her feet and legs as she scuttled down the ledge and ran toward the horses. The blanket grabbed on brush around her, but she gripped it and pushed it up off her legs, around her shoulders.

As she ran she heard somebody clattering behind her. She cut hard right, stumbled over a bush, and went down with a crash.

"Resa! Come back. You gut-stuck Badger."

She waited a minute. Yet the wet cold of the morning clawed at her. The scrapes on her legs hurt. Dawn was coming up and with it her realization of what she had done.

"He dead?"

"No, but he's bleeding like a stuck pig."

Slowly she walked behind Garcia, back to the ledge, wrapping her blanket around her. Shivering. Uncertain.

"Bitch. All I wanted was a little!" Badger howled when he saw her.

"And I warned you not to mess with her. She gave you just what you deserve," Garcia reminded him.

Resa climbed into the cave. In the pale light, blood splattered, green-red, on the floor. Boone stood over Badger. Badger was holding a rag over his belly.

"Get your clothes, Resa. We're going."

"But . . ." Badger sputtered.

"Do as I say, Resa. Badger did his work, now he can take his pay."

"You can't leave me! Christ, I'll bleed to death." Badger's eyes widened with alarm.

"Maybe so, maybe not."

"But, we've been friends."

"'Friends' just ended."

Resa was terrified of what she had done, and of Badger's face—desperate, pleading. She was terrified of Garcia's coldness. She threw on her clothes. Wordlessly, she helped Boone pack, trying not to look at Badger's eyes, at the blood oozing out from between his fingers.

43

"I'm leaving you one canteen. Your horse."

"Please, I didn't mean it. Please." Badger crawled toward Garcia.

"Come, Resa."

She stared at Badger. She felt pity for him. Garcia took her hand, nudged her toward the ledge.

They got to the horses and saddled and packed them. Neither said anything about the swearing, then the keening that drifted down from the cave.

"For a kid, you're sure as hell good with a knife." He swung up into the saddle.

"I didn't mean . . ."

"Come. I left him his gun."

She rode blind, tears flooding her eyes. As they picked their way toward the valley, she shook her head. She wiped her eyes on her sleeve and straightened her shoulders. The day passed, warm and cloudless. She prayed for forgiveness. She prayed for Badger, her prayers mixed with hate and fear. Still, a chill gripped her. There seemed no absolution possible.

Chapter Three

The sun was high on the new-washed world when Garcia motioned to her to be quiet. He dismounted and she followed as he led the pinto to the edge of a clearing. On the far side of the clearing, which had once been a pasture, but was going back to nature, she saw a ramshackle adobe cabin, behind which was a stable. Behind it were some disintegrating corrals, their cross-posts fallen or teetering against the uprights that slouched toward the sandy soil.

They stopped and watched silently. The heat rose in waves off the grass; Resa felt stifled. She was curious about the house. Above them a flight of sparrows scattered and resettled in some cottonwoods behind the building. She could see chipmunks skittering across the road in front of the house. Otherwise all was quiet.

Her horse pawed nervously, yearning for the grass.

"Careful, now," Garcia said, and swung back into the saddle, starting out into the clearing.

They rode their horses behind the house, dismounted, and let them drink from the spring that bubbled there. Through the trees that sloped toward the valley, Resa saw a creek. They took the saddles off and hobbled the horses, letting them graze. They entered the house through the back and fumbled around in the darkness, opening shutters.

They stood in a confusion of men's leavings—a moldering pair of boots in one corner, bits of rock-hard crumbs on the uneven slab table, ashes from a pipe stuck to a pottery dish that was the ashtray, a deck of cards strewn out on the table. Other decks were stashed in the niches on the adobe fireplace. A couple of sheepskin jackets were tossed in a heap, along with some other clothes, on a buffalo robe that smelled musty. It lurked like an evil presence on the hard-packed dirt floor.

"It smells like a stable," said Resa.

"Welcome home," he said. Garcia dropped his share of the gear on the table and Resa dropped hers on the floor. Unable to tolerate the smell any longer, she rushed to the front door, then the back, opening them wide to let in air.

"Tear up some old shirts around here and clean the place up some while I check our supplies. Maybe we can go fishing later."

"I love fish, Mr. Garcia."

"Call me Boone."

For several hours the dust flew. After Resa dragged everything that she could—the stinking robe included—out onto the grass, she felt more at home than she had since the massacre. Doing something familiar brought back the memories of Milledgeville, and of how her mother's maids did things in the vast plantation mansion. For a while she was a kid following Tildy and Elspeth around with a dust cloth and broom as she had in the days before they were freed and her mother clumsily took over their jobs, cursing them for leaving, cursing the war that had forced them to leave.

Only once or twice did Resa think of Badger. She cried, then, soundlessly so as not to distract Boone, who wandered in and out with loads of provisions which he produced—flour, sugar, beans, an extra frypan, a couple of pots.

In mid-afternoon, he started a fire, and Resa helped him make a pot of beans.

"We can do biscuits when we get back. Mike left a sourdough to start on that shelf," Boone pointed out. "You know, Resa, this place looks fine. Nothing like a woman's touch." He looked at her critically, then said, "Grab that bar of soap. Let's have a bath."

Resa stood frozen in her tracks. "You won't hurt me?"

"Course not, partner. I'll just show you where we go, then I'll hightail it up the creek and look for some trout. I got some worms from out by the stable."

Resa didn't trust Boone, but she was terrified to be without him. "You won't go far?" she asked.

"No. But there's not much to worry about except for a bear now and then or an Indian or two."

Her eyes were huge.

"Can't you take a little kidding? You know I won't leave you. If it'll make you more comfortable, we'll take the gun."

"Fine . . . let's go."

Boone showed her where to bathe—a fine, deep hole at a bend in the creek. He left the rifle on the bank with her. Taking his pistol, he went upstream, not looking back.

The water was so cold it stung her skin blue. Resa squealed as she plunged in. Every few seconds she looked nervously around. Finally, she gave in, lathered her hair, and dared to close her eyes long enough to wash it well. The soap was so strong, she felt it practically taking her skin and hair as well as the dirt, but she reveled in her cleanliness.

She got out, dressed in Peter's second set of clothes, combed and braided her hair, then bent to wash her trail-worn clothes. When they were finished, she draped them on the bushes to dry, picked up the rifle, and started up the creek.

"Boone! Boone!" she called. Rounding a bend, Resa saw him. He motioned to her to be quiet. In an instant his fishing line grew taut and he hauled in a ten-inch trout—the latest of four. He strung it with the others on a willow twig.

"I'm going for a bath, now. Try your luck for awhile. Don't take them all, though," he smiled.

She picked up his pole—string rigged on a new-cut willow branch with a worm-covered hook tied to the end—and let it drop onto the water. The sunshine bathed her shoulders and soothed her. The creek chortled down its course. Resa settled into a revery. Boone seemed kind, yet he killed Mike and left Badger to bleed to death. In his dark appearance, there were similarities to her brother Peter. Dear Peter. She and Peter had been such good friends. When he wasn't with the boys in the neighborhood, hunting or such, Peter often took her fishing. Unlike the other boys, who thought girls were sissies, good only to sit around in their dimity dresses playing dolls or embroidering, Peter liked her company. He put up with his friends' teasing so she could tag along.

Boone didn't look much older than Peter. Yet he was. Sometimes he acted very old. Resa wanted to know about Boone. About everything. She'd ask him where they were going, what they were going to do. She'd not think about the past. She'd pretend it was a dream, that she was a princess in a fairy tale who awakened one day in a new world with new flowers, new trees, new people. Then she wouldn't think about her family, she wouldn't remember.

Resa caught one fish, adding it to the string. Then they stopped biting. After awhile, she gathered up the fish, the pole, and the rifle, then went back down the creek.

She rounded the bend near the hole. Boone was lying on the grass, barefooted. His shirt was off and he was staring up at the treetops. His holstered pistol rested just to the right of his hand.

"Boone?" He turned toward her and smiled. His deeply tanned face contrasted sharply against his white, black-haired chest.

"You're striped like a skunk," she laughed.

"You look pretty as a butterfly. Amazing what soap and water will do."

Her cheeks blazed. "It didn't hurt you any either. I'm hungry. Let's go back and fix these." She held up the string. "I only got one."

He slipped his mocassins on, then put on his shirt. It was white. She hadn't seen a white shirt since they left Milledgeville. They gathered up their clothes and started back to the adobe.

"We staying here long, Boone?"

"For awhile. I've got to go to Las Vegas soon."

"Can I go with you?"

"Sure. We're partners. Just one thing. If I take you, will you promise you won't try to run out on me?"

"Where'd I go?" she replied. "What do you need in Las Vegas?"

"I'll be trading. Here, you take the rifle and clothes in while I gut these. Put some flour in a pan, and find some bacon. It's in the stuff I set on the table. We'll fry these up and make us some biscuits."

By the back door, some columbine was blooming. As she went past it, Resa picked a few flowers. With the spring nearby, she didn't mind wasting water. She put them in a tin cup on the table. Her mother would have liked to know she wanted flowers. In Milledgeville, even after the war, her mother kept the place full of them. She never let them die in the house. Except for the wagon, the house in Milledgeville was the only home Resa had ever known. Now this hovel was home. It still stank. She remembered everything about their plantation up river, as though it were right outside the door. Sometimes on the trail she missed it, but she had a family then, and visions of a new ranch in Santa Fe. Now this was home, and she didn't know where this was, and she knew nothing of the man who had started calling her "partner" except that he had killed one man because of her and had left another to die. She slumped down at the table and started to cry. She couldn't make sense of anything. She was homesick. Lonely. Afraid.

"Hey, where's that bacon?" Boone entered with the fish. Finding Resa in tears, he set the fish on the stove. Boone let her cry while he fished out the bacon and rustled up some flour.

"Look, missy, I know it's hard," he comforted her, "but will you try to keep from drowning your flowers?"

The tears coursed down her soft cheeks as Resa said, "It's just I don't know where I am and I almost murdered somebody this morning and now Badger's probably dead and I was thinking about what it's like back home, and I miss my folks, and . . ."

"Tell you what," he said, and handed her a handkerchief. "You dry up. Help me with dinner. Then I'll tell you something about this country, about myself. Now grab that fry pan."

After dinner, Boone took out his pipe and tobacco. They sat out in front of the cabin.

"I never talk much about myself," he said.

He drew on his pipe. Resa pulled at the grass, arranging it in little nests around her. The sunset, red and gold as molten iron, silhouetted the pines and cedars across the meadow.

"My mother was, in some ways, like yours. She was pretty and, like your Ma, I think, a lady. She and my Pa homesteaded in Ohio, she told me. He was killed by Shawnees, and she moved west when I was tiny, to Crooked Creek, in Missouri, between Independence and St. Jo. She was a schoolmarm. She taught me lots of things. Everything she could. She had a great thirst for learning and she passed it on to me.

"When I was about eleven, she got a fever and died. The town elders sent for my Aunt Ophelia and her husband Edward. They took me to their farm just outside St. Jo.

"Well, they had six kids of their own to feed. Their kids hated me. I was smarter than they were in school, and being raised off a farm, I didn't know how to do chores, so they gave me the worst ones—cleaning out pens. You ever had to keep hog pens clean?"

Resa's eyes were wide with interest. Like a child at the knee of a storyteller, she shook her head no.

"My uncle had no use for me, either. I wasn't much help and, to him, I was just a no-count mouth to feed. He saw no use in book learning and despised me for knowing how to read and write and for wanting to learn. He caught me reading a book I'd brought home from school one time when I was supposed to be working, and he beat me silly with a bridle he'd been mending.

"So I ran away to Independence. I didn't know much about how to make a living and I got pretty hungry. I was fishing garbage out of some barrels behind the Trail's Head Saloon one night when this woman, Sally, found me and took me in. She owned the Trail's Head, and she started me off sweeping floors for two meals a day and a pallet in her storage shed."

"So, you're an orphan, too," Resa interjected.

"Yeah," Boone sighed, "but it's been so long, I don't think of it anymore."

"Then what did you do?"

"Well, I stayed with Sally for a long time—several years. As I grew up, I learned lots about how to make money. Pretty soon I was making my own."

"How?"

"I learned gambling. I was good at it. Still am."

"Why did you leave?"

"Sally and I had a falling out in '63. I pulled out of her place. Opened one of my own parlors down the street. That rankled her. She claimed I owed her money. I thought she owed me for all the years I'd put in for just my board and room.

"Anyhow, after the war there was a new sheriff, who thought there were too many bars in town, so he closed me down. Left me broke."

"But how'd you get in cahoots with Mike and the others?"

"Well, I started out for Santa Fe just about as poor as when I ran to Independence. When I got to Raton Pass, it was a scrape for me to pay the two dollars and a half it cost for me and my pack mule to go down the pass. I was sitting at Wootton's Station trying to figure out what to do when Mike and some others came riding in. We sized one another up. They needed a gun hand, I needed a stake, so I threw in with them. We've been riding up and down the Santa Fe Trail from the pass to Las Vegas."

"Just like the wolves in my dream," Resa shuddered.

"It fed me. Got me a stake. If I were you, I wouldn't be too critical. Anyway, Mike and I stashed our stuff here. You might say we were collecting it until we each had enough to go on in style. After we left here, last trip out, we picked Badger up. He doesn't know the way here, so don't worry. He won't be following us.''

"I wish I hadn't had to stab him," Resa shivered.

"Hell, even puppies bite when they're threatened. Don't let it worry you." Boone stood up.

Inside they bedded down. It was stuffy after he closed the shutters. The buffalo robe, on which they both lay, was a forgiving mattress. Slivers of moonlight pierced the shutters.

For the next three days, they worked around the cabin. Resa found a needle, thread, and scissors. She set to work mending, patching even the smallest tears in her clothes. Then she did Boone's.

Resa discovered that she was good with sourdough. The second day, she made two loaves of bread while Boone busied himself in the stable, currying the animals, mending tack.

She made bacon sandwiches with the warm bread. She picked flowers and took a blanket out to the meadow in front of the house. When the cups of coffee and sandwiches were arranged on the blanket with the flowers, she called him.

"You're a fine cook," he said, as he sampled the sandwiches. "But a poor tactician. In the middle of this meadow, we're a clear target for anybody."

"I didn't think," she said.

"Next picnic, let's go down by the creek. There's cover over there."

The wine of the mountain air soothed Resa. Each afternoon she peacefully fell asleep. But she had nightmares and her screams pierced the cabin. Each time she awakened, Boone was always there smoothing her sweat-soaked hair back from her brow, patting her, offering her water. Yet once she was awake, he moved away and acted as if nothing had happened.

The third day, after she cleaned up the breakfast dishes, he said, "I'll need your help today, partner."

They went outside. Boone was never without his pistol. Today, he took the rifle as well. They skirted the meadow, walked down behind the spring and along the creek, then went back to the stable. "You keep a lookout," he said. "When I get this cache open, you can help me unload it."

He took a spade and pushed it under the dung-heaped floor until it hit wood. Resa was torn between watching outside and watching him. Boone started flinging manure to one side, and soon it was shoveled off a wooden door two feet by four. He pried around the door with the shovel, loosening it. Then he wedged the handle under the door and pulled up, revealing a wooden cache, four feet deep. At the bottom was a large, flat iron box. He climbed into the pit, and lifted it out.

"My books."

Resa gave up looking out. She turned to Boone and opened the box. Inside was a canvas pocket. She opened it. Shakespeare, the Bible, Byron, and the Romantic poets lay before her, their pages slightly crinkled from dampness, yet their leather covers were in pretty fair shape. "Oh!" she cried happily. "I haven't seen books since Georgia. Books!"

Several smaller metal boxes filled the rest of the hole. Resa put the books aside and stared into the pit. Boone opened one. Gleaming from the rusted metal were small bars of gold.

"Mother Mary, a treasure!" Resa gasped.

"We hit the Bloodstone Mine bullion train about a month ago. We were waiting for another the day those fools decided to attack you instead." He started lifting the boxes out.

"Stack these in the stall with the horses, against the wall," he said.

"Just like in fairy tales," she murmured.

"This fairy tale got five or six people killed. I'll be glad to be away from here."

"How much is it worth? What will you do with it? Oh, Boone," she sighed, "we're rich! Rich!"

He stared coldly at her and she shut her mouth.

There were six boxes in all. After she stacked the last one against the wall, he brought out a small oilskin sack and showed Resa the jewelry that Mike had gotten on an earlier heist. He left the pit, closed the door, and shoveled the manure back over it. Then he took his horse, and led it over the area until the floor there looked like the rest of the stable floor. Then he walked to the back of the stable, grabbed some empty sacks and a full one, and arranged them around the gold.

"Let's have some coffee," he said.

Back inside, Resa poured coffee. They both reeked of the stable, but this time she didn't care.

"There's enough there to make you a fine lady, and to set me up in business," he said.

"If we talk about it, it'll disappear," she said.

He laughed. "I forget what a child you are sometimes." His dark eyes held her gaze. She shoved back her fright, and stared back at him.

"Let's get the stench off," he said. "Last one in the creek's a dirty thief!" He grabbed the rifle, and ran out the door. She raced him. They unbuttoned buttons as they ran. Yet when they neared the creek, she veered away from the hole, and charged through the grass upstream, laughing.

After they were clean and had dinner, they settled in front of the cabin. He read Shakespeare to her. She read him some Wordsworth, some Coleridge.

"Tomorrow, I go for deer," he said after she finished "The Ancient Mariner."

"Can I go?"

"Sure . . . a few more days we'll be tradin' in Las Vegas. Then we'll ride into Santa Fe like we own it."

A jay called from a nearby tree. He looked at Resa. She was asleep in the sunshine. That day, that night, the nightmares stopped.

The next morning Resa was so excited about the hunt that Boone had to tell her to be quiet several times as they trailed up the mountain behind the cabin.

"Pa and Peter always said hunting was man's work," she chirruped.

"If we get a clear shot," he promised, "I'll let you try for him first—although it goes against my common sense. I don't want to spend the day tracking a wounded animal or scaring up another if you miss."

They rode high up above the adobe where a string of alpine meadows footed the base of a crumbling mesa. In the dewy shade of the trees, Boone hunched up his shoulders; Resa didn't seem to notice the chill. They passed the narrows between the first and second meadows. He saw plenty of signs of game, and motioned for Resa to be ready, as he pulled to her one side. He checked the air. It was barely moving downslope. Silently as cats they dismounted, tied the horses to some aspen saplings, and walked down below the meadow.

Like ghosts they moved through the aspen grove. At the edge, he looked out. Above them, fifty yards off, stood the herd—ten deer—milling around a spring.

"Try for a small doe," he barely whispered.

She took her time, sighting a doe in the Remington. She concentrated, and glanced at Boone as though wishing his finger could be on the trigger. Her eyes were huge. She wiggled herself into a solid stance, sighted again and squeezed off the shot.

In the chaos of flight at the end of the meadow, he wasn't certain, momentarily, whether she'd hit one or not. Then he saw the body drop. A young doe.

"Good shooting!" he yelled to her as they ran toward the kill.

"I did it! I really did it. I did it!"

The bullet had gone right through the neck.

"Resa, you're something else."

She followed him with the rifle while he dragged the carcass down the slope, toward the horses. When they got to the trees, he hoisted it up on an aspen, and tied it.

He opened the cavity carefully. Dipping his fingers in the blood, he motioned to her.

She stood before him as he put the blood on her cheeks and forehead.

"Now you're a properly initiated hunter."

She reached up and kissed him, standing on her tiptoes. Then she went dancing away from him, bending and whooping in circles like an Indian. She whirled past him again and again, feinting at him, full of herself, the deer, the day. Boone reached out and grasped at her pigtails. Her wild dance went on until she was out of breath and giggling.

She stood panting several feet away from him, her cheeks and forehead flushing under their strain, a crazy kid's grin on her face. Then she rushed past him again. As she did, he grabbed her hand and, laughing at her laughter, drew her to him.

She tensed like a cat—every muscle fighting to spring. He lightened his hold, stroked the blood from her cheek. He put his fingers lightly on her lips.

"Resa, you're special. I know you've been hurt, but *I* won't hurt you."

She ran her hands along his arms, eyes closed.

He kissed her eyes. He kissed her hands. She was trembling like the aspen leaves above their heads. He drew her to the meadow grass.

"I care," he whispered. "You're my beauty," he said as he nuzzled the nape of her neck.

With one hand he stroked her chestnut hair, and with the other he unbuttoned his shirt.

Resa tickled his face with the end of her pigtail. Yet she was shivering. He drew her tightly to him, rubbing her legs, arms, back, as though to warm what he knew was not cold, but fear. At last, she warmed toward him.

Resa pressed her hands against Boone's chest, and stroked his thick mat of dark hair. A tangle of emotions knotted in her breast for she was alone with this man, a man who killed, a man who gambled, but—she was certain—a man who loved.

Carefully and slowly, Boone unbraided Resa's pigtail, transforming her from a pretty child to a lovely woman. His hands circled her back and sent arcs of desire through Resa.

Soon the meadow was alive with their love.

Chapter Four

Five days later, Boone and Resa rode into Las Vegas, trailing the two mules. Wooly's horse, an evil-tempered gray, held their cooking gear, clothes, and food. He was in poor shape.

In their saddlebags, they carried the gold and Mike's jewelry—rings, necklaces with precious stones and pearls, brooches, cameos, silver combs, and hair clips. Boone had Resa's teak box.

They tied up at the general store.

"Remember," he reminded her, "you're my niece, if anybody asks." They dismounted.

"Good we hit here when the town's asleep," said Boone as he stared down the street.

Resa felt frightened. Flies buzzed around fresh cowpies in the dust-choked street; they lit on the horses, on the dogs that lolled swish-tailed in the shade of doorways along the street. In the corrals down the way cattle bawled against the heat. By a watering trough in front of the saloon across the street, five pigs cooled themselves in the mud. Yet there were no people on the street. Chickens scratched in the middle of the road. The town was deserted.

They walked into the general store. It smelled of cinnamon and tobacco, of leather and sawdust. Jars of candy, bins of beans and flour, strings of dried red chilis captured her eyes, and fought for her attention. Yet, the store was empty.

"What you mean, coming in during siesta?" Through the curtains that separated the store from what Resa assumed was an apartment, a fat man with a tobacco-stained moustache came. He wore the pants of a heavy wool suit. Whatever he had eaten for the past few weeks was splattered on them. A dirty white shirt bloused outside them.

"We need some things," said Boone. He was edgy.

"You must be new in town. Nobody in Las Vegas buys at this hour. Damned heat!"

He brought out three bottles of sarsparilla and opened one. Boone nodded. He opened the others and gave them each one.

He stretched. "I'm awake now. You say you need things?"

"Yes. Clothes, mostly, some flour and chili powder." Boone walked to the window and watched the animals.

"Clothes. For yourself?" He turned to Resa.

"Yes."

She followed him to a dark corner of the store. On tables were piles of fabric, mostly calico, boxes of shoes, a few felt men's hats, and a pile of buttons and thread in a jumble in a glass bowl.

"This ain't Saint Louis," he grumbled. "We ain't got much ready-to-wear. Mostly girls like you sew their own."

"She hasn't been where she could," said Boone. His eyes never left the street.

"You got any skirts?"

"Here's a gray wool. Serve ya well through the winter."

She held it against her. It was too big. Like everything else she looked at, it was a jumble of wrinkles.

"Cotton, please. And smaller."

He dug down in a stack of skirts, and produced a hideous calico with purple flowers on a green checked background.

"No. In a plain color." Resa wrinkled her nose.

"Fussy, ain't ya?"

"The lady has a right," said Boone.

The clerk shrugged. His eyes shifted to the man at the window.

"This better?" He found a navy blue cotton skirt. Underneath it was a gray one. He hauled them both out.

She put them against her. They would fit all right; although they were a little large around the waist, the length was suitable.

"I'll take them. Now show me some shirtwaists."

While he dug through another pile, she went to the opposite end of the counter. In the gloom, she found a huge pair—the only pair—of pantaloons. She put them aside. With a needle and thread she could baste them so they'd fit. She pawed through some hats. Underneath them was a stack of undergarments—camisoles and petticoats. She found one plain camisole she thought would do, and a muslin petticoat, rumpled and dirty. Yet she put it with the pantaloons.

"Here's two. Only ones left, by the look of it."

.She held them up to her shoulders. The first was huge. The second must have come to Las Vegas for a wedding and been abandoned. It was a beautiful shirtwaist with a deep, ruffled yoke and long sleeves with ruffles at the cuffs. It was too fancy for her needs, but she loved it.

She gathered everything up on her arm and took her goods to the front of the store. Boone relaxed his guard as she showed them to him.

"That petticoat looks like it's been used as a saddle blanket," he said. "I'll give you three-fifty for the lot. Dirty as they are, you're lucky to get that."

"This ain't St. Louis," said the man.

Boone ignored his comment and asked, "You have shoes? Gloves?"

"I said . . ."

"This ain't St. Louis," Boone finished the sentence. "Just get me two pounds of coffee and chili powder."

Resa watched out the window while Boone paid.

A drunk stumbled out of the saloon and veered around the trough. Off balance, he started for the hitching post where their animals drooped in the heat. He seemed not to notice them. He came right toward the rump of the evil-tempered gray.

The horse seemed to sense the drunk's distance. When the drunk staggered within range behind him, the horse let go and sent the drunk sprawling back to the middle of the street. The gray sashayed sideways and kicked at one of the mules, who brayed loudly. The mule pulled to the side, hitting the one next to him, who honked as he hit the second mule's hind leg with his.

Boone and Resa ran out to the street to settle the animals.

"Moose turds!" The drunk scratched his head. He staggered up and ran limp-legged up the street, veering through the chickens.

"Let's get out of here before the sheriff arrests us for disturbing the peace," said Boone.

Resa looked at him. They laughed and went back to collect their things.

They traded the gray and one mule for cash, then left.

"He was right," said Resa as they made

their way out of town. "Las Vegas *ain't* St. Louis."

The three days' journey went easily in spite of Boone's worry about their load. They were sitting around the campfire the last night out.

Boone chewed on a straw, and said, "I've been thinking . . . when we get to Santa Fe, I'll be putting you in school."

"School? I know how to read and write. That's all I need. Pshaw, back home half the girls my age are married already, or most will be by next year."

"I don't want arguments. If there's a boarding school, I'll put you in it. Otherwise, you're going to whatever school there is. You know a lot about surviving out here, but Santa Fe's another thing. You'll need a trade."

"But, I thought—oh, Boone, marry me, marry me."

"I'm a gambler. We lead dangerous lives. Keep strange hours. What will you do while I sleep all day? You'll sit around tapping your foot, waiting."

"But, I love you." The statement shocked Resa almost as much as it shocked Boone.

He was silent a moment. Then he sighed, "I know. What kind of a man would I be if I didn't take care of you the best way I can figure?"

"But . . ."

He reached out and drew her to him. He tousled her hair. "Santa Fe's a new world, Resa. It's beautiful. Mexican. Dangerous. A beauty like you's got to know how to live tough, or you'll make mistakes that can land you in trouble. I can't be with you like now, so you'll have to take care of yourself most times. My life's not for a lady."

"If you marry me, it won't matter." Tears filled Resa's eyes. But the hardships of the trail had taught her determination. Just as she willed away memories of the massacre, she willed away her tears, and swallowed hard.

Boone intruded on Resa's thoughts. "I'm not a marrying man. I am what I am and we have to live with it."

They made love under the starry sky that blanketed the frontier. Resa wondered, as Boone held her, what the next days would bring. Yet the day had been long, and she drifted to sleep, too tired to worry about the future. Boone moved away from the fire and watched through the calm night, occasionally slapping himself awake. Yet nothing stirred. Not even Resa. He was glad. Her nightmares had troubled him more than he wanted to admit. He watched her, sleeping like a baby, her lips bowed as though she were kissing something. He admitted he was in love. Yet he knew himself for a loner, so he pushed the thought away.

In the morning he made coffee and wakened her. "Let's get a move on. It's only three hours. We'll eat when we get there."

While she packed up their bedrolls, Boone slapped the packs on the horses. They rode out quietly, each in his own thoughts. Ahead of them was a freight wagon, behind was nothing.

"Let's not sit here." He eased the pinto into a steady trot. Her sorrel followed. Soon the sunshine and anticipation of the city, the steadily increasing traffic—a wagon train of ten wagons coming in, more freight wagons and a mule train going out—made them feel excited.

Santa Fe. As Resa and Boone topped a rise on the trail, it lay before them, shimmering in the August heat, dusty and fetid with the stink of its stock and its sewage. The city was a dun, bruised stone perched on the blue diadem of the Sangre de Cristos. They passed through a broken, heaved-up collection of adobe shacks with round outdoor ovens that skirted the walls of the presidio. Outside the gate, a pack of mangy dogs lolled in the sunshine. Inside they were attacked by the noise of blanket peddlers, squash vendors, and wagons pushing through the crowds, their riders swearing at the congestion. The plaintive wail of a streetsinger's Spanish; the arrogant English commands of a rancher, hustling several men out of a bar; the child voice of a boy hawking squirrels in rude cages billowed up a cacophony of sound, which played against the motionless quiet of Indian women, sitting on the boardwalk in front of the Palacio, in the shade of the wooden arcade, selling melons, baskets, and pottery.

From the center of the plaza came divine, spicy odors, reminding Resa she was hungry. Yet they rode past the confusion, through a narrow alley to a livery stable, where it seemed an eternity before a dark-eyed man waited on them.

"Everything takes time here," said Boone. "The Spanish don't move as fast as we Yanks. Help me, Resa, will you?"

They removed the saddlebags. Boone made the stable boy understand he wanted help. They unpacked the mules and carried the gold down the alley. They made two trips while Resa waited with the jewelry. Boone paid the boy well. Then, laden with the last of their luggage, they walked down the alley into the side door of a large adobe building that faced on the plaza—La Fonda.

Her boots felt uncomfortable against the terra cotta tiled floor, and her eyes took in the whitewashed perfection of the gypsum-painted walls as they contrasted with the massive dark wood beams of the ceiling and the stairway leading upstairs. Silver candle sconces lined the stairway, set in niches in the walls. High above her a huge silver chandelier amazed her. Again, the smell of something delicious made her faint with hunger.

Several gentlemen took their leisure in the lobby, puffing on cigars. One was reading a newspaper, another studied his watch expectantly, then rose—a smile on his rotund face—as a woman, dark and stately in an embroidered green dress of some marvelously sheer cloth came down the stairs, a dark-suited boy in tow. Resa remembered that she hadn't combed her hair. She was conscious of her dirty shirt and Peter's baggy linsey-woolsey pants, of her chapped sunburned skin and her thick leather belt.

"Room's rented."

"Hungry as I am, I'd sooner have a bath."

Boone laughed. "A bath it is." He arranged with the desk clerk to send water up. He dug in their gear, retrieving their clothes. Laying them on the counter, he requested that they should be quickly cleaned, pressed, and delivered.

"We'll go out in style. This evening, I'll show you the town. Tomorrow I start working." Boone took her elbow and steered her upstairs.

Later, when they were dressing, Boone admired Resa in her blouse and skirt. "Now, if we can just find some shoes to replace those boots, you'll be the prettiest girl in Santa Fe." He reached in his pocket and abruptly said, "Here."

She looked down at the object he thrust into her hand. It was a delicately-wrought oval of gold in the center of which was a small amythyst—her mother's.

Resa gasped, "It's beautiful! I'd forgotten." She ran to the window and pushed back the curtain to study the brooch's violet/blue sparkling in the sunlight.

She glanced across the street. For an instant, just turning the corner, she thought she recognized a familiar figure as it disappeared. *Badger!* She jumped back from the window, dropping the pin.

"Whoa! What was that all about?"

"Nothing. Skunk just crossed my grave." She brushed the thought from her mind while she crawled on the floor, under the bed where the pin lay.

Boone helped her find it. He hugged her, caressing her newly-combed hair.

"As soon as we get settled, I'll give the jewels back."

"Fine. But I can't eat them. I'm starved. Let's go."

They gorged themselves on steaks, rice, beans, and fancy cakes. Afterward, they took a leisurely tour of the town. Patiently, he waited for her while she prayed in the church on the square. Her prayers were a bubbling mixture of thanks, penitence, and promises like the whirling promise of the day.

They passed a blacksmith shop, several stores selling household goods, clothes, and hardware. One small shop on the edge of the square especially took her eye. They strolled inside. It was a millinery, filled with hats, bonnets, delicate underthings, shoes and gloves.

"Oh, look!" she exclaimed as she donned a yellow hat with a large red flower on her curls. She pirouetted in front of Boone.

A dark-eyed woman asked to help them. She was well-dressed in navy, with pince-nez.

"You make these hats?" asked Resa.

"Yes, most of them."

"My niece would like some shoes and gloves." Boone cut into the conversation.

"I've the perfect ones here," said the clerk. From a display case, she produced a pair of black high-topped shoes. "Fine quality. From Boston."

"They're ugly," said Resa. "I'd rather have these. She pointed to a pair of black satin evening shoes.

"Try the others. The mud will ruin the satin in no time," said Boone.

She tried them on. They fit fairly well.

"May I have the others, too?"

"Quit teasing, Resa. They're not suitable."

"Your niece is forward," said the clerk. She looked at Boone with a raised eyebrow.

"Lost her manners on the trail."

"All right," Resa gave in. "I'll take the ugly ones."

"I like a spirited girl. If you want to learn to make hats, I could use an apprentice," said the clerk.

"I'd love that."

"My niece will be in school," Boone said, glaring at Resa. "Perhaps later. After we're settled. Now, how about some gloves?"

"Right here." The woman produced a pair of white cotton ones with a row of tiny pearl buttons at the wrist.

"It's silly for *me* to wear them."

"Not silly at all. Your uncle wants you to be a lady."

While she tried on several pairs of gloves, Boone browsed around the shop. He brought a plain navy blue straw hat with a long grosgrain ribbon flowing down the back to the counter where Resa stood. He put it on her head.

"If you fancy this, you may have it."

She looked at herself in the mirror. The plain hat was too plain for her. She visualized herself in the fancy yellow, or a maroon one which was bedecked with mounds of gray feathers, but she knew better than to ask for either.

"I look like a school girl," she complained.

"Then it's perfect," Boone said. "We'll take it."

The clerk said, "My name's Julia Estanza. If you decide to work for me, you can find me here every day except Sunday." She addressed Resa, yet her eyes fastened on Boone's face as she spoke.

Boone paid. They finished their tour. Soon they were walking along a row of saloons. Loud guitar music came from inside. A sign of a crowing red cock swung above the door. "Can we look?" Resa asked.

"If you promise never to come near."

Her eyes were huge as they stepped into the gloomy interior lit by candles.

Along one wall stretched the bar, crowded with a variety of men in various degrees of drunkenness. Behind the bar was a huge painting of a naked woman surrounded by paper roses. Card tables filled the remainder of the room. At the far end of the bar two women in bright red skirts with low-necked blouses sat with some wranglers. Their bosoms hung loosely beneath the thin cloth. Their eyes were painted with black paint; their mouths were tinted, too. Resa recalled a day when she and her friends in Georgia read about harlots in a book her cousin stole from her father's library. They had sat on Rosa's bed reading, giggling over their adventure.

Now they were here.

She felt worldly, but her bubble burst when Boone drew her back out the door.

"Is this where you'll gamble?"

"No. I'll only play at the best tables—La Fonda, a couple of the better saloons. I play strictly for high stakes. Fact is, I plan to build my own place soon."

"I can't imagine us away from the cabin."

"I know. Thank God the riding's over. I

hate horses. If Santa Fe weren't so wild, I'd have a carriage and driver.''

Resa walked in front of him and turned to size him up. In spite of his dark suit and clean white shirt she couldn't imagine him as anything but a trail-wise drifter.

All her life she thought of him like that, sweet with the smell of cedar and sweat, stroking her back at midnight, laughing with her as he taught her games on the buffalo robe.

Chapter Five

In September, Boone steered a reluctant Resa into the adobe school house that sat on a pine-covered hill above the city.

"I don't *need* school."

"You *need* better manners," he said quietly as he steered her in the door. He removed his hat. The room smelled of chalk and ink. Flies buzzed around the windows.

A potbelly stove—cold in the late summer's heat—stood next to a huge wood box. A large slate hung behind the desk. At the desk sat a pale woman in a gray dress. Her hair was done up tightly behind her head in braids. Yet she was startlingly pretty—not like any schoolmarm Resa had ever seen. She rose when they walked in, and Boone introduced themselves.

"I'm Miss Patricia McShane," said the teacher, taking Boone's hand. "Come, let's sit down."

"My niece was orphaned when her family was moving west," he began. "A massacre by Indians. She wants to continue her education."

Behind her desk, Miss McShane could not see that Resa kicked him on the shin. He smiled and applied pressure to her elbow.

"Poor child," said Miss McShane. "It must be terrible for you."

"Since Uncle Boone and I have been in Santa Fe, I do feel lonely," Resa said. Boone relaxed his hold.

"Garcia. Boone Garcia. You're the man who's building the new 'saloon'?" Miss McShane eyed Boone curiously.

"Yes."

Miss McShane slightly raised her eyebrows and asked, "Do you read, Resa?"

"Yes. Everything. Well."

Boone quickly added, "She needs more training in mathematics and in history."

Resa rushed to tell the teacher, "I'd like to own a shop like the millinery on the plaza when I'm grown."

"I . . . I'm not certain." Miss McShane blushed at Boone. She fluttered her eyelashes, seeking the right words. "The other parents . . . your line of work . . ."

"Surely you will accept Miss McCutcheon," Boone said smoothly. "I plan to make a large contribution to the school. I favor education. My mother, God rest her soul, was a teacher."

Resa stepped on Boone's shiny black boots. Hard. Again, he applied pressure to her elbow.

"It's done, then. Welcome, Miss McCutcheon. We'll expect you on Monday." She stood and shook hands with them both.

"I didn't know you could lie so pretty," Resa glared at him when they walked away from the school. "What's so bad about a saloon, anyway?"

"I didn't know you could step on my toes so pretty," he said, throwing his arm around her, withdrawing it quickly. "Uncles shouldn't be seen hugging their nieces in public."

Resa groaned.

That night after the tables at La Fonda emptied, Boone allowed himself one of his two daily bourbons at the bar.

A well-dressed fat man with a shock of white hair and a heavy gold watch chain glittering on his dark suit purposefully pulled up a seat next to him.

"I'm T. J. Pryne, Mr. Garcia. The banker where you have your business."

"I remember."

A bar girl came up behind T. J. Pryne, she hugged him.

"Buy a tired girl a drink, T. J.?"

"Get, Gloria. I'm busy." He patted her rear as she walked off. She wiggled her tail at him.

"I admire your business plans," Pryne turned his attention back to Boone. "Fact is, I'd like to be your partner."

Boone tersely replied, "Had some partners once. I don't want any more."

"I could be silent. Just put in the money, take my share. Surely you can use more cash."

Boone turned toward Pryne. "I plan the only parlor house in Santa Fe. I've enough. I don't need your help."

"I can make it hard on you, Garcia."

"Try it and get your ass broken. Now, if you don't mind, I'll finish my drink alone."

"Fine," he said, and paused. "For now." Pryne blustered out of the bar. Gloria made an obscene gesture behind him as he left.

"Who is he?" Boone asked Gloria.

"Nobody. He likes to be able to throw his weight around. Nobody takes him seriously."

He bought her a drink and finished his.

"I've two more girls lined up for you," said Gloria.

"Fine. That makes six. When I open, are you planning to be my madam?"

"I told the boss I'm leaving. He didn't much like it, but he knows I want to get ahead."

"Good. Three more months ought to do it."

He left and walked from La Fonda to the church. Behind the church, across the street, he looked at the board and adobe shell that stood half-finished in the moonlight. *The Golden Web. That's what I'll call it.* He whetted his appetite, imagining what it would look like when it was finished. Then he walked back toward the inn. The streets were deserted. Far down a side street a piano tinkled faintly. It was growing cold.

Suddenly he thought he heard something, sensed something. He drew his .44 and dropped into the doorway of the church. Yet he could see nothing nor hear nothing but the piano. *Skunk crossing my grave*. He moved cautiously into the street. Nothing.

In the weeks that followed, Resa got more and more restless. Boone was always either working on the saloon or sleeping; it seemed. They laughed in their loving. Both found it hilarious that she should come in from school and jump into bed with him before they ate dinner and he went off for the night. Yet, one night he came in and found books thrown all around the room.

The next day was Sunday. Resa went to church as she always did, leaving Boone asleep. He wakened in mid-afternoon.

"Resa," he called lazily, rubbing his eyes. "Get fancy. Today's the grand show of the club. I've planned it just for you."

Silence.

He got up and dressed. Still, Resa did not come back. His watch read three o'clock.

By four o'clock, Boone was in a lather. He'd thought of every place she might go, every trick she might pull to make him angry. And he was worried.

He paced back and forth, wearing a path through the room.

At four-ten, Resa quietly let herself into the room. She carried the rifle and was wearing Peter's clothes.

"Where the hell have you been?" Boone demanded angrily.

"I went hunting," she retorted. "Got to do *something* to pass the time."

Boone strode before Resa and gripped her shoulders. "What a damnfool thing to do! You had me worried." He searched her eyes for remorse.

Resa slapped his hands back and spat, "I can take care of myself. Can't sit here all day!"

After an angry pause, Boone snapped, "Get dressed. We're going to the saloon."

"That damn place." She started undressing, throwing her clothes helter-skelter around the room, scattered with the books.

"Don't swear," Boone admonished her automatically.

Resa's fury peaked, and she shouted, "Don't hunt! Don't swear!" She was breathless with her anger. She paused, then added softly, "You'd think you were my uncle or something."

Boone caught her glance a moment, and said calmly, "Let's not spoil the day. I want to show you everything. It's just about ready."

Resa silently put on her clothes. She

pouted as they walked to the saloon. Boone let them in.

Her curiosity got the best of her bad mood. Soon she was ferreting out every corner, looking behind the mahogany bar, examining the tables, and staring at the lanterns that hung from the ceilings and walls. To the right of the bar was a double door. She opened it and ran through the room, up the stairs, then down again—her hand resting on the polished banister. Boone stayed below listening to her light footsteps. She bounded in front of him.

"It's a, an assignation house isn't it?" Resa stared straight into Boone's black eyes.

"No. It's . . ."

"Don't lie to me, Boone Garcia. Lying to Miss McShane's one thing, lying to me's another."

Without a moment's pause, Boone answered, "Yes, it is."

"You are disgusting . . . how many girls will be working here?"

"Six at first."

Resa was sick with fear and suspicion. In a flash, she saw Boone delighting in the ladies while she sat in class. She asked, "How many have you tried out?"

"None."

"I said, don't lie."

"Resa, I'm not lying." He stared down

her look of disbelief. He crossed the room and put his arms on her shoulders. "There's only you."

"For how long? How long until some girl comes in here who turns your head?" Tears welled in her eyes.

He stroked her arms. "God knows, I hope never. Sometimes, when I'm with you, it's enough to make me wish I'd never learned this, but I don't know anything else. I need money. I like living well. I've no intention of changing until I can make a bigger bundle at something else."

The tears brimmed over Resa's lashes as she whispered, "I feel so helpless. You've treated me like a two-year-old ever since we've been here."

"It's not true." Boone wrapped her in his warm embrace.

"But I'm out of your life. I'm just a dumb kid with no place to go."

"If you were dumb I could stand to see you in the life. Truth is, I've kept you away from this because it's not pretty. There's a better future for you. Be patient."

"Patient! All I do is sit around with nothing to do. I've read almost all the books in the school library; when I go out to hunt I feel spooky. You're fussing over this place all the time. I'm lonely."

Strong emotion gripped Boone as he said

fiercely, "Don't ever leave town without me again. You hear me?"

"You can't stop me," Resa said petulantly.

"No, but you can. You know it's dangerous. Have some patience. Soon I won't have to work so much."

"Soon will be too late." Resa tilted her head back and said, "Listen, I decided this afternoon that I'll go back to Mrs. Estanza, ask if I can apprentice myself to her at the millinery."

"All right. It'll be good training."

"Keep me out of your way, you mean."

"It was your idea, damnit," Boone said impatiently.

She started to cry. "I'm just so alone. I hate it. My family. My friends. Now you. I'm so alone."

He kissed her neck. "Sometimes I forget how hard it's been. Forgive me?"

"I guess so. But don't ever lie to me again."

"I want to protect you. I want the best for you."

"I can take anything but lies."

"It's good the truth's out. No more."

"I hate it—what you do." She sighed. "But I love you more."

Chapter Six

Boone was shaving the next afternoon when there was a knock at the door of their room.

"Señor Garcia, there's some women downstairs wanting to see you," said the desk clerk.

"Thanks, I'll be down presently. Did they say what they want?"

"No, but there's six or eight of them."

"Wonder what this is all about?" he said to Resa, who stared questioningly at him from the desk where she was doing her schoolwork.

He dressed meticulously. "If I'm not back in ten minutes, you'd better come save me."

From the stairway above, Boone could see the women. He'd not realized there were so many prissy Anglo women in Santa Fe. It seemed to him every pearl-decked stout lady in the city must be waiting for him. *God, I'm not even open yet, and here's the morality committee.* He pulled on his tie as he descended the stairs.

"Mr. Boone Garcia?" The white-haired woman, corsetted from her toes to her neck beneath her navy blue dress with its ropes of pearls, had a stance that reminded him of a Sioux chieftain's. Her feet were set solidly on the ground, dug in for a long parley.

"Yes. May I have your name so I may have the pleasure of addressing you?"

"I'm Mrs. T. J. Pryne, this is Mrs. W. T. Bullard, Mrs. Brent, Mrs. Benton, Mrs. Smythe, and Mrs. P. L. Trease."

He surveyed them. One nervously clutched her handbag to her ample bosom, one had a head of white braided hair that stood so high he was amazed; one, stringy with thick glasses and a droopy bosom full of pearl buttons atop the powder blue of her dress, flushed crimson when he looked at her. The others were younger, but no less blue-nosed.

"What can I do for you ladies?"

"It's come to our attention that you're co—cohabiting with a young woman, a student at the school," Mrs. Pryne said.

"She's my niece," Boone explained without a smile. "Her family was killed and she was delivered to me in Las Vegas before we moved to Santa Fe."

"We know the nature of the establishment you're constructing, Mr. Garcia. We feel St. Theresa's orphanage would be a more suitable place for your 'niece,' if that's what she really is."

"He's lying," one woman whispered loudly. "My family in Las Vegas never heard of him."

"Madam, are you impugning my character?" asked Boone. "Were you a man, I'd take you to task for this slander."

The woman's face reddened. She stared at her toes.

Mrs. Pryne's jaw merely jutted further out from the fat rolls of her neck.

"An orphanage would scarcely be the place for Resa. We're family. It's a point of pride with me to discharge my obligation toward her."

"Yet, in your line of work, we feel you'll have a corrupting influence upon her," stated Mrs. Bullard.

"My 'line of work,' as you so delicately put it, Mrs. Bullard, has nothing to do, I assure you, with my relationship to my niece."

"Yet we've ascertained from the clerk of this hotel that you're inhabiting the same room."

"Disgraceful," whispered Mrs. Brent.

"Honi Soit Qui Mal y Pense," said Boone.

They stared at him as though he had sworn, their expressions disquieted, their campaign crumbling beneath his breeding and charm.

On the periphery of the delegation, now, stood a group of interested bystanders, men who had come into the lobby and who had gotten caught up in the scene. They looked on with amusement.

"Your high-falutin' language does not impress us, Mr. Garcia," said Mrs. Pryne. "If you do not alter your living arrangement with Miss McCutcheon we will demand that she be removed from the school as a bad influence."

"We like to think of ourselves as being very tolerant in Santa Fe," added Mrs. Brent, "but we can not have her teaching our daughters bad examples."

"And has she been teaching your daughters—your children—lewd things?" asked Boone.

"Not thus far, but given her circumstances, it's just a matter of time." Stringy Mrs. Benton withdrew a handkerchief from her handbag and delicately blew her nose.

"As you know, ladies," Boone remarked coolly, "my establishment will open for business this week. I have given some thought to the matter of my living arrangements with Resa and had decided, at that time, to purchase a house, to hire a duenna to look after her. Naturally, I will not be living with her, as my interests keep me occupied at odd hours."

One of the men in the surrounding group guffawed.

"Naturally, as I'm certain Resa would welcome companionship among her schoolmates, it would please me greatly if, at that time, you would allow your children to associate with her. Her family was a fine one of wealth and breeding from Georgia. I'm certain you'll not cast the offspring of such good people into limbo."

"Don't waste your breath on these bid-dies!" Resa stood on the balcony. "I'll do what you say, Uncle Boone, but not because of this meddling."

"Hear, hear," some men in the group called.

Without saying another word, Resa stalked back toward their room. From their vantage point, the people in the lobby couldn't see her blushing cheeks nor the tears on her face nor the fury that knit her brow. *Why didn't he tell me we were going to live apart? What will I do without him?* Furious, she threw a vase against the wall. It shattered.

"The arrangement you describe will be acceptable," said Mrs. Pryne. "Mind you, don't live with her anymore."

The women turned to leave.

"Oh, Mrs. Pryne. You should know that your husband expressed great interest in my place. In fact, he offered me a partnership, but I turned him down."

As the women, shocked, in disarray, retreated to the street, laughed out of the room by Boone's parting sally, he reflected that he had won—but he wasn't so sure about Resa.

Yet when he consoled her she understood. Resa was so desperate to keep Boone, she relented. "If you visit me often, it'll be all right I guess."

He dried her eyes and helped her pick up the pieces of the vase.

Late in the afternoon Boone was helping the carpenters install the mirrors he had bought for the walls at the saloon.

"Boone? Boone Garcia?"

He turned and climbed down from the ladder.

"Well, I'll be damned! Charlie Kelly." The men shook hands.

"I thought it was you with Pryne," said Charlie.

"What brings you from Independence?"

"It's getting too civilized. I was out for buffalo this summer. When fall came on, I drifted down this way. What the hell are you doing here?"

"Sheriff Smith locked up my place. Last spring, it was. By the time I got the girls and me out of jail and gave them something to get them down the trail, I was broke. Smith's with Sally now. Guess she didn't want any more competition. You want a drink?"

"Does a buffalo have a hump?" Kelly joshed.

"You'll be initiating my place," said Boone as he poured them whiskey.

"She's gonna be a dandy," Kelly said as he admired the polished wood and gleaming crystal of the bar.

"Best house east of San Francisco, I hope. Once I get my nudes for the walls."

They raised their glasses. Kelly was a huge man. One of Garcia's best customers in Independence, he was a talkative character, a spinner of tales, a kisser of the Blarney stone. Yet he had been a sniper with the Union Forces. When he got riled, his enemies cleared out pronto.

They had another drink.

"What you plan on doing here?" Boone asked.

"Haven't made up my mind. Maybe mule skinning."

"Why don't you work for me? I can use a bouncer. It's warm in the winter. You can have all the company you want for free, as long as you don't keep the girls from the paying customers. You can eat here. Bunk in the extra room upstairs. I'll pay you a dollar a day."

Charlie shook Boone's hand. "I'll take it. A cat in a field full of catnip!"

"Let me show you around." They took their drinks. Charlie appreciated the bar, the faro wheel, the new-poker tables, but he was ecstatic over the house.

He tried out each of the red overstuffed loveseats in the parlor. He plinked a few chords on the battered piano, pronouncing it beautiful. He admired the vermillion draperies, the brass fittings, the silver chandeliers in the parlor, but when he followed Boone upstairs, he was really in the height of his glory. He bounced on each of the mattresses. "If they can hold me, these beds can take anybody," he said. "Lord-amighty, what a place!" They skipped a tour of the kitchen. Boone didn't think Charlie would be interested.

"I'll be moving my gear in right away," said Charlie as they left.

The next day Boone left Charlie to help the carpenters. He found Resa a house on a hill to the north of the main part of town in a tree-lined narrow street that wound its way toward the Palacio. Like the other houses on the street, it was small, built in Spanish style around a courtyard in the center of which was a shrine to the Virgin. On the wooden arcade that ran around the courtyard, Virginia creeper—red with autumn—choked the pillars.

"I love it!" exclaimed Resa. "It's perfect."

The hard-packed dirt floors yielded nothing to their shoes. Resa touched the walls. Whitewash came off on her finger.

She chirruped a list of furnishings as they walked through the parlor. "Oh, look at this crazy door."

They stood in the dining room. The entrance between it and the kitchen was roughly man-shaped, chiseled out of the two-foot thick adobe walls.

"It's the shape of a ghost," she said.

They laughed.

"With curtains and rugs, plants and some plain furniture—a sofa, two or three chairs, a bed—it'll be home. May I have a bird for the patio?" she asked happily.

"Soon. First we've got to find you a watchdog."

"Watchdog?"

"A duenna. The Spanish keep old mean women around to help with the housework sometimes, but mostly they just look after the unwed girls to see they don't get into any trouble."

"Does she *have* to be old?"

"It won't be easy finding a young one. They're all busy raising their own families. I'll see what I can do."

"Since she's going to live with me, let me pick her," Resa pleaded.

"Okay, but I'll have to approve of her. I'll

ask around anyway for you and see if I can come up with a choice. I'll get Charlie to help us move. The stable's good, too—for privacy."

Resa giggled, "Don't bring any more treasure."

The day before the saloon opened, Boone bought three finches in a tall cage from a street vendor, taking them to Resa to mollify her. He'd barely seen her for the three days. After they got her settled, he and Charlie moved into the parlor house.

"I found a duenna, today," Resa said after thanking him for the present. "She lives right down the alley. I saw her with some children this morning. They were playing tag—she and the children—down near the shrine at the end of the block. She was good with the children—laughing, playing. She brought apples for them. The way she cut them for the children made me like her so I talked to her. A mixture of English, Spanish, signs. Anyway, I found out she has just lost her job. She'll move in with the kids next week. She'll cook and keep house."

"Kids? How many? Where's her husband?"

"Wait. First things first. She's thirty and

her name's Maria Sanchez. She's not married, as far as I know. The kids belong to her sister, who's cooking for the summer. It'll be fine. The kids will stay here sometimes, but mostly with their mother. Maria has kind eyes and she's Catholic."

"She's too young to make the morality committee happy. You can bet your life they'll be watching, too."

"Pah. She's fat and not pretty—she's missing three teeth in front—and she's more Indian than Spanish. She said something about Santa Domingo Pueblo being her home."

"All right," Boone relented. "We'll give her a try."

"I made her understand that when you come here, she's not to bother us. She's to keep her mouth shut."

"I'm glad she's Indian. If she were Spanish soon she'd tell somebody else's servant, who'd tell somebody else's servant about us. With an Indian that's less likely."

Resa hugged Boone and rested her cheek against his chest. "How I wish I could be there when the saloon opens," she said, hoping Boone would say yes.

"There's no way I'd let you."

"Do you ever feel some strange force looking over your shoulder, making your neck hairs stand up as if a grizzly bear were breathing on them?"

"No."

"Sometimes I feel it. Today after school I stopped in the grocery by the wagon yard. There's that tall rack of baskets back in the corner. I could swear somebody was looking at me from behind them, but when I went to see there were just the baskets."

"It's been a busy week, Resa. Moving. You feel it again, though, and you let me know. With Charlie around there's no need to worry. I can have him follow you if you want."

"No. It's probably just my imagination."

Chapter Seven

Winter closed in. The winds howled down from the mountains. Snow blanketed the city. People huddled near their fireplaces. The streets were all but impassable. A sea of mud, frozen in ruts in the morning, became an icy hog wallow in the afternoon. When they went out at all, people tied rags around their shoes in a futile attempt to save them.

Yet spring was all around Resa as she made summer bonnets, sitting near the fireplace at the back of Estanza's millinery.

She was sewing a yellow silk rose on a fawn-colored straw hat one afternoon when Boone came in.

"There's a break in the storm," he said as he came to the back. "Mrs. Estanza says you can ride with me for an hour if you want."

"I'm so glad you are here," Resa said as she sprang up. "Look at what I've made." She took him around the work area—piled with material, showing him her creations.

"They're fetching. You're an artist, little one."

"Here's my masterpiece," she said, holding up an immense dark blue felt with sequins and plumes sweeping along the wide brim. "I love it. I love it so much I want it for myself."

"You'd look like one've my girls in it. It's much too old for you. Still, I could buy it for you if you promise not to wear it until you're thirty."

She laughed. "By then it'll be moth-eaten, and I'll be a wrinkled hag." She looked down at her skirt. "I'll ride in this if I can ride astride. I hate sidesaddles."

"Fine. Charlie's waiting. He won't care,

and there won't be anybody to sneer."

Charlie heaved a sigh of relief as they came out of the store. He was sheepish even to be hitched in front of a ladies' shop.

They rode to the benches behind the city, muffled against the wind. Charlie rode behind them. He was always with Boone now. There had been vandalism at the casino and threats against Boone.

"I admire your work. You're becoming real independent," Boone said.

"I think how my mother leaned so much on us. I'm determined to make something of myself, that's all."

"The idea of having a business is good. When you're ready, you can have your mother's jewels. They'll buy a lot of calico and felt. Still, sometimes I wish you could stay a child."

"I can't." She looked back at Charlie. "And gamblers do live dangerously." She reached across and kissed him.

"Don't worry about me. Nobody's likely to see me dead before I'm eighty. I've been thinking. In a couple years I may pull out of the house. Go somewhere and start clean. With railroads coming, the future looks bright."

"Now that Maria's nieces and nephews are gone, I'm going to teach her to make hats, too. Can I have some money for material to teach her?"

"You've really taken to her."

"Maria's all the friend I need besides you. Last week she spent a whole evening telling me all about the winter dances at Santa Domingo. We . . ."

Charlie rode up by them. "If it's all the same to you, I think we should be heading back now. I don't like Pryne's threats."

"Sure."

"What about Pryne?" asked Resa. "Isn't he the husband of that lady who came to take me to the orphanage?"

"After I turned him down on a partnership, I found out he's one've those who doesn't like to be shut out of anything. The other night he and some of his boys were playing poker with me. I cleaned him pretty good at five card stud. Upshot of it was, he got mad, then he got drunk and threatened to burn me out. I can't be gone long.

"The word's around that he's hired some new boys. They're supposedly just new hands for his ranch, but I've heard a couple of their names before. Gunslingers."

"You ever feel like we were safer when we were on our own?" said Resa.

"No. You just were too scared to know how bad the danger was."

"Still, I liked it then. Just you and me in that cabin," Resa said wistfully.

"I'm a civilized man, Resa. Not even you'd ever get me back on a farm. Let's go."

The raw wind was blowing harder. By the time they trailed into Santa Fe a blizzard had started.

"No need to worry about Pryne in this," Boone yelled to Charlie over the fury of the wind.

"Still, I'll be glad when Resa's home."

After her ride with Boone, Resa was pensive. Maria tried to get her interested in a game of poker, but instead she sat gazing hard into the fire. For the second time that week, as Boone and Charlie escorted her up the steps to the house, she felt the "thing" that occasionally haunted her.

"What bothers you, give it to *Nuestra Señora*, no?" Maria said as she turned toward her bedroom early in the evening.

"*Si. Nuestra Señora.*"

In the lantern light of her bedroom, palely illuminating the bed that was too flat without Boone, Resa removed her crystal rosary from the hook on the little sanctuary of St. Francis. Boone had given it to her for Christmas.

She said her rosary, kissing Boone's pillow beside her . . . "Please keep him safe.

110

He's sinful, I know, but I love him. He's so kind to me. Please, don't let Pryne hurt him."

Then she put out the candle and the lantern and fell asleep. The wind howled with the fury of a widowed Apache squaw.

An icy chill woke Resa. She glanced toward the window rubbing her eyes. A hulking shape blotted out the faint window light. It loomed in the fire's glow. She was wide awake, reaching toward her bedside stand where she kept a derringer. Yet, faster than she, the hulk moved, knocking the stand to the floor. Her favorite ivy fell, its pot shattering. The noise brought Maria into her room.

"No more games," said the intruder.

"Badger?"

"Yeah. Tell your girl to get us some light. Just one candle, you hear?"

Resa told Maria. Her voice squeaked in her throat.

"I'm back. Yeah. I didn't die when you left me. I've spent every minute since then waiting. Waiting 'til Boone got good and fat. Waiting to kill you both. To get rich."

Maria came in with a candle. Badger took it from her. "Now get across the room where I can keep an eye on you."

Resa shivered as she stood beside Maria.

"Get dressed," Badger snarled. "We're going for a ride."

"But the storm. We'll freeze to death."

"Shut up. Do what I say."

Resa rushed frantically around the room, throwing on as many layers of clothing as she could find, dragging them on under her nightdress, then adding a heavy skirt and blouse and jacket, while Badger sneered at her. Maria glared at Badger.

"My coat and gloves. They're in the other room."

"Fine."

She went into the sitting room. The hall tree was right by the front door. The door that would lead her out into the patio where she could shout for help. Badger, pushing Maria in front of him followed her. Escape was so close. Help was so near. Yet Resa didn't dare try anything or Badger would shoot Maria.

At last she stood ready.

"Your girl speak English?"

"Some."

"Tell her to go to Boone when she gets untied. She's to tell him to go to Torreon Cantina. The barkeep there knows where we'll be."

As he said it, he tied Maria to a chair with his lariat. She spat. She swore, struggling against the ropes.

"Now git," he snarled at Resa. They went out the front door onto the snow-heaped patio. He prodded her toward the stable where he'd tied two horses.

Resa's own horse whickered as she mounted the one Badger had brought. "Sorry," she apologized to him.

"Shut up."

They drew out of the stable, the horses hunching in on themselves against the savage blasts of the wind. Resa drew her muffler up over her face and pulled her hat down. In ten minutes their tracks would be covered. She was filled with pain of the cold and hatred of the man. The clotted dirty beard covering what had once been Badger's boyish face left her no doubt that she was being taken by a madman to God knew what mad place. *He's like a ghost. A ghost that can't rest until he's killed us. God forgive me, I should've gone to confession. Maybe it would have released him.* Her hands, covered only in light kid gloves, were already numb.

They rode past buildings that she recognized on the north side of town, but once they were past the hovels on the outskirts of the city, Badger turned. They headed into a trackless waste. Soon she had no idea what direction they were following.

The blizzard let up. They could see a little although it still snowed. The horses stumbled in the deep snow. Near dawn, he stopped her and let her pee. Badger tied a handkerchief over Resa's eyes, then led her horse by its reins. He said not a word, nor did she. She'd rather have died than let him know how frightened she was.

The wind stopped. Her legs and arms sensed that it had stopped snowing. In the blackness of her isolation, she silently swore every curse she'd ever heard; she even invented some.

At last they stopped. He helped her down from the saddle and led her into what she knew was a building, for she heard him unbolt the door. Inside, he stamped his feet. She was left standing there.

"Can I take this thing off now?"

"All right."

She took the blindfold off. They were in a shack—probably a line shack, for it had chaps, lariats, and spurs hung on pegs. It smelled of horse.

There was one chair. Badger dragged her to it and tied her numb hands behind her back.

"There. That ought to keep you outa mischief."

He started a fire in the corner fireplace, then went outside to tend the horses.

It was an hour before Maria got herself untied—an hour before Boone and Charlie got the message at the cantina.

After Boone and Charlie left the Torreon Cantina, they conferred for a long time. Badger's message was that Boone was to ride to the line shack, alone. He was to bring twenty-five hundred dollars if he wanted to see Resa alive.

"I know that place," said Charlie. "It's flat out in the open south of here—nothing for two miles around it except a little bluff maybe a quarter mile away."

"I'll be a sitting duck," said Boone.

"Yes. But if you're willing to take a chance, I have an equalizer. You'll have to get him outside the cabin, clear of it."

Then the blizzard came up again. Boone and Charlie could do nothing against it. Boone drank the day away in his room—he was mean as a grizzly with the snow and the waiting. He yelled at the cook, who brought him dinner. But he ate it, along with two pots of coffee.

Early the next morning, long before dawn, Boone rode by himself to the south.

The light snow slowed him some, but the wind was gone. Black clouds wallowed above the Sangre de Cristos, but the moon was out.

He saw the shack some two hours later. As he and Charlie had planned, he had arrived just at first light. Relieved, he found there was no wind. The hair rose on the back of his neck as he rode directly toward the shack. He felt as foolhardy as he seemed.

When he was about a quarter mile away, he drew his pistol. Fired it into the air. Slowly. Cautiously. He kept riding toward the shack.

"Badger! Badger Pearcy!" he called at last.

"I hear you," called Badger.

"Don't hurt him," shouted Resa. "He let you live!" She was straining against her ties. Blue bruises raised above her eyes where Badger had cuffed her.

"I have to keep you alive 'til he comes," he had said. "I don't have to keep you pretty." He'd hit and hit her until, in spite of her determination, she had cried out for him to stop. He just laughed at her while he hit her some more.

"Yeah, missy," he grunted between blows.

"After I get the money I'm going to kill Garcia, but not before he watches me cut you into little pieces. Slow-like."

"I've got your money!" shouted Boone.

"Good. Now, drop your gun."

"Let me see the girl first."

Badger untied Resa. Holding the pistol to her back, he pushed her to the door's edge.

"C'mere sucker," he mumbled as Boone dropped his pistol, making a display. Then he reached in a bag to show Badger the money.

"You're gonna have to come out for the money. I'm not getting closer," Boone called out.

"Drop the sack," Badger said.

To Boone's satisfaction, Badger came out of the shack, gun drawn and pointed. Wary as a cornered cougar, Boone watched him come.

Badger shot. Boone fell, wounded. His eyes focused on the outcrop in the distance. *Shoot, damnit, shoot!* He waited for a puff of smoke.

"You're crazier about her than I thought," Badger spat as he rushed toward Boone, gun poised for a coup. As he stood six feet from Boone, Boone heard the unmistakable sickening thud. A huge hole gaped in Badger's chest. His knees buckled. Rasping, he fell forward. The report of the rifle filled the air.

Inside the cabin, Resa pulled at her ropes. She was certain Boone was dead. "God! Oh God! Help me!" she cried.

On the bluff Charlie raised the rifle in triumph and let out a whoop and did a snow-choked jig. He was proud of the shot that had dropped Badger. "That Sharps is a honey," he smacked his lips. The way he had sighted in the rifle, resting it across his saddle blanket on the rocks of the bluff, was good. Combination sights worked perfectly. He had gauged it well.

Chapter Eight

Charlie rode into the area in front of the shack. He knew that Badger was dead. But he was cautious anyway, as he dismounted near Boone. Boone was semi-conscious—hurting, by the looks of it.

"Where'd he get you?" said Charlie.

"Here," Boone groaned.

"Who thought up this damn fool stunt,

anyhow?" said Charlie, as he opened Boone's jacket and shirt, confirming that the shot had lodged just to the left and below Boone's neck. "An inch or two either way, and you wouldn't be here. We just damn near didn't make it."

"Help me up," said Boone.

Inside the cabin they heard wailing.

Charlie helped Boone to the cabin. He untied Resa who had pushed the chair to the floor in her struggle to get free. She bounded up off the floor and ran to Boone, tears streaming down her bruised face. "My God, my God. I thought he killed you!" She reached under her shirt and pulled off her cotton petticoat. Methodically, she set about ripping it up for bandages.

"He's bleeding bad," said Charlie, looking at Boone, who lay on a rat's nest of a bed in the corner. "Here. Give me those rags. You look around for anything we can use to pack this."

"Turn around," said Resa.

When Charlie was turned, she reached into her corset top and brought out some cotton she used to round out her figure. "This isn't very clean, but it'll have to do."

Charlies dressed the wound, Resa looked on with tears running down her face. They stung her bruises.

"Doc will have to take out the slug. How're you doing, Boone?"

"It's been better," he wheezed. "Let's get out of here."

"You lie still for a few minutes," Charlie said. "Try to stop the bleeding some. There any coffee around here, Resa?"

"Yeah, but not much else. He didn't figure he'd need much. He was going to kill us both and hightail it back to town. Said he'd collect from Pryne before he left."

"Pryne? That doesn't make sense. He hired those gunhands. Why'd he let a two-bit punk come after Boone?"

"Maybe he figured if Badger got me, no one would suspect Pryne put him up to it." Boone's breathing was shallow. "Now we'll call out his big guns. The way Badger messed up Resa, I'd like to take them all on."

"Not for a while."

Resa made coffee. As soon as they finished it, they got ready to leave. Charlie helped Boone into his saddle; he helped Resa, too. By now her eyes were swollen almost shut. Her arms, her legs, her gut—they all hurt.

As they rode all she could think of was taking care of Boone. He'd need nursing and she was going to provide it. She and Maria would move out of the house. Maria could help her with Boone.

They limped back into Santa Fe, Charlie nervously watching, hand on his pistol, for any more attackers. People on the streets stared at them. Boone's slouch in the saddle and Resa's black eyes caused a furor on the snow-choked streets.

They rode around the back of the house. Charlie helped Boone up the steep stairs to the second floor. Resa went ahead of them to open the door.

At the top of the stairs, Gloria DeSanza met them. *"Dios mio!"* she cried, brushing past Resa as she went to meet Boone and Charlie.

Resa reached out and spun Gloria around. "Don't touch him. I'll take care of Boone. If you want to help, you go for the doctor. Then go for Maria. Tell her to bring clean clothes and my night clothes and come pronto."

"What's a kid like you know about nursing a man?" Gloria asked.

"What I don't know, Maria does. Do as I say," Resa commanded.

"Resa, you can't stay here. Gloria and the girls will take care of me," said Boone.

"Over my dead body," said Resa.

Charlie laughed.

Resa turned down the bed while Charlie

helped Boone out of his clothes. The girls gabbled around the door to the bedroom like so many clucking hens, until Resa shooed them off, telling a couple of them to draw water for a bath.

She poured water from the bedside stand and gave Boone some. Meanwhile, she gathered his clothes, put the ruined ones aside to be thrown away and stacked the others in his wardrobe.

Boone lay bleeding onto the towels she'd put on the bed.

"Resa, I know you mean well, but don't you think it's better if the girls and I take care of him?" said Gloria.

"He's my man. He saved my life."

"Let her stay," mumbled Boone. He reached out his hand to her and smiled weakly. She took it, soothing the skin with her fingers, kissing it.

Charlie went to stand guard outside the room, closing the door behind him.

"You've got spunk, kid. *Nobody* talks to Gloria like that." Boone chuckled, followed by a cough and a wince. "You look like hell," he said to Resa. "How're you feeling?"

"I'll be all right . . . truth is, I feel rotten. God in Heaven, why couldn't Badger just leave us alone?"

"If it weren't Badger, it'd be somebody else. In Independence there was always somebody wanting a piece of me. Guess it's going to be the same way here. Up 'til now I've been lucky. Never been shot before." He closed his eyes.

"If only it didn't have to be like this."

"I am what I am. No use trying to change it."

Resa put his hand to her bruised face. "I know. I know."

A knock at the door brought the doctor and Charlie who insisted she leave. She stood in the hallway with its smells of cigar smoke and bourbon and stale perfume and soap. She heard Boone moaning behind the closed door. It seemed ages before the doctor and Charlie came out.

"He has a broken collarbone. The bullet lodged beneath it. We got it out but there are bone chips left in there. Now he's gonna be all right if we can avoid an infection," said the doctor.

"He was a handful to hold down," added Charlie.

"Who's going to be tending him?" the doctor asked.

"I am," Resa said determinedly.

"Keep him warm. Give him lots of water and broth. If he starts running a fever, sponge him off and let me know. Later we'll have to see about getting those bone pieces out."

"Charlie?" Resa asked, "where's Gloria?"

"I'll find her."

Maria came in the door then, carrying a suitcase.

"Jesus Maria!" she said when she saw Resa. She dropped the suitcase and rushed to Resa, taking her in her arms against her big bosom. "Tell me."

"Later. Now, you help."

Gloria came down the hall, rearing to reclaim her control over the house.

"What you want?" she asked sullenly.

"I want you to clear out the room next to this one. Maria can help you. I want to be as close to Boone as I can."

"That's Rita's room," Gloria objected. "She's my busiest girl. You can't."

"I don't care if she does business in the hall," Resa insisted. "I want that room."

"You know what I do to girls who talk like that to me? I fine them plenty." Gloria pushed her face right into Resa's.

"I'm not one of your girls! You don't have to move Rita out, I'll see Charlie moves her."

Charlie watched from the end of the hall. "Jesus, keep me from the carryings on of

125

women," he sighed.

"I'll see Boone pays you for Rita's inconvenience," said Resa.

That mollified Gloria. "Maybe I can put her at the edge of the landing," she said as she strolled away, shrugging her shoulders.

"Maria, after you've helped Rita move her things, go to the kitchen and find out where my bath water is. See they bring it up quick. While I bathe, you watch Mr. Garcia."

She made up a pallet in the corner of Boone's room. He slept fitfully, although Resa couldn't understand how he could sleep at all in the noisy house.

Left by herself with Boone asleep, she studied his domicile.

The walls were covered with calico, the rough floors with fabric called gerga. The ceiling was made of wood beams, behind which smaller lengths of wood met the beams in diagonals. In the corner sat a huge desk, littered with all manner of papers, a box, a bottle of whiskey, and two glasses. On the shelf above the desk was a mantel clock of brass with a china face and brass hands pointing to Roman numerals. A desk chair was swung casually away from the desk. Next to the desk was another straight-backed chair at the base of which rested a brass cuspidor.

On the deep windowsill behind muslin curtains, sat several plants in terra cotta pots.

To the other side of the room, a corner fireplace held a hot fire. In two niches in the wall above it were Indian pots. In front of the fireplace over the gerga was an Indian rug with red, brown, and white lightning in its design. To either side of the hearth stood a wood box and tools.

On the wall to the left of the fireplace sat a wardrobe of some dark wood. Next to it was the bed—a large wooden one with heavy carving at head and foot. Boone had told her about it. It was his pride and joy, a purchase from a Mexican trader. It was covered with a Mexican blanket in all the shades of the rainbow. To the left of the bed, a gun cabinet, containing the house's arsenal, sat ponderously next to the door. On the other side of the door were some crude shelves on which were stacks of papers, a large bottle of ink, quill pens and books.

Boone awakened and struggled, moaning, to sit up.

"I'm thirsty," he said weakly.

Resa poured him a glass of water from the pitcher next to the bookshelves. When she touched him, he was hot. His skin felt dry.

She wrung out a rag and applied it to his forehead.

"It's like ice," he said. "I hate it."

"Shhh." She bathed him again and again.

"I hate fever. It reminds me of my mother."

"It's all right. You're not going to die."

"Of course not," he said. Then he rolled away from her and went back to sleep.

Yet by the next afternoon Boone's fever was much worse. "Get whiskey. Get Charlie. Get a bartender or somebody to help me hold him," said Doctor Manning, when he checked Boone's wound early that morning. "I'm going to have to get those pieces out now and sterilize that wound again, or we'll lose him. Give him this opium. It'll quiet him. I'll work on him as soon as he's drowsy."

"Charlie and I'll hold him," said Resa.

"You sure you can take this? It's not gonna be easy."

"It'll be harder standing outside," she said. She gave Boone the opium and went to get Charlie and Maria.

After Boone was drowsy, Dr. Manning probed for the chips. Boone moaned. When the doctor splashed whiskey onto the wound, Boone let out one terrible scream, then he passed out.

"Don't leave him alone," said the doctor as he bandaged the wound.

"As if I could," Resa said, her brow wrinkled with worry.

"If he makes it until morning, he'll probably be all right."

The clock above the desk became a world in which Resa lost herself. She wandered between the hands, so tired she barely knew reality, her ears fastened to every breath Boone drew. "Tick. Tock. Tick. Tock." Every stroke of the clock took her to some place she and Boone had been together, every breath he drew was a slender thread, linked to the clock's ticking that drew her toward him. She and the clock and her memories of Boone became a power, praying him back from death. Yet he lay as though dead, and Maria and Gloria had a terrible time making her leave the room when they came to relieve her while she went down the stairs to the kitchen for the meal they insisted on.

As though wrapped in the life and death struggle above them, the girls sat around the kitchen table silently eating. They looked up when she entered, expectantly.

"He's still alive," she announced tiredly.

Ordinarily, the mounds of potatoes and

beans, of tortillas and peas, the platters of steaks resting on bright Mexican dishes would have been cheering. As it was, the display of food made Resa's stomach recoil. Yet she knew she must eat something, so she studied the women and the room as she toyed with her food, distracting her mind from Boone.

All of the women were dressed in housecoats of bright fabrics with flounces and furbelows. One, a tall redhead that somebody called Cindy, pushed back her plate and lit a small cigar. Next to her sat Rita and Nita, twins dressed in identical purple robes, their hair piled high in pompadours with turtle shell combs. Gloria sat at the far end of the table. She had on a yellow dress, cut fashionably low over her heaving bosom. At the base of her cleavage a large amethyst pin rested. Resa had to admit that she was pretty. To her right sat Becky, a blond freckle-faced girl no older than Resa, whose pale blue dressing gown sat uneasily on her shoulders, too big and too fancy for her child's face. Next to Becky was Martha, an older woman with great mounds of fat unconcealed beneath the bright red tent of her robe with its lacy tiers. Her brown hair, too, was piled high, revealing large golden hoops that drooped from her sagging earlobes.

"What you staring at?" she snapped at Resa as she shoved the peas toward her.

"Nothing. I'm just tired."

"Ain't you never seen a whore before?" Nita lisped, batting her eyelashes in Rita's direction.

"Shut up," said Gloria.

Resa stared down at her plate, poking the food in.

"Why, you've got a shiner bigger than the one Sourdough Pilchard gave me last week," said the red-head sympathetically.

"That still don't make it right for her to be here," said Rita. "I can't do half the business I usually do on that landing. Noise makes me nervous."

"Leave her in peace," said Gloria. "Get on out there and get busy."

The cook, an Indian woman, shuffled over from the stove and started clearing plates. The women pushed back their chairs and left.

"Don't let them bother you," said Gloria. "They're as worried about him as we are."

"Not likely," said Resa.

"You're all right, kid." Gloria patted Resa's shoulder as she went toward the parlor.

Chapter Nine

When she wasn't bathing him or fighting with his body as it restlessly thrashed in the bed, Resa spent the night pinching herself, humming, stretching to keep herself awake. Maria came in at two, begging her to sleep, but Resa wouldn't leave.

Near dawn Boone moaned. He opened his eyes and looked around. Resa bounced out of the chair and felt his forehead. The fever had broken.

"Water," he croaked.

"Thank God! Thank the Virgin, thank St. Francis! You're back!" said Resa. She held the glass to his lips.

"Told you I wouldn't die," he smiled wanly.

"Shhh. Sleep now," she said. As soon as his eyes closed, she pounded softly on the wall of the adjoining room. Soon Maria came in, sleep hanging heavily on her puffed face.

"You stay with him now. Fever's down." Resa squeezed Maria's hands in hers. "Don't wake me until afternoon unless he gets worse."

In the days that followed, Boone steadily grew stronger. Resa read to him from the plays of Shakespeare and from the poetry of Poe and Byron. She especially liked *Don Juan*, and she and Boone spent hours laughing over the antics of that sly lover.

One afternoon, three weeks after the shooting, Resa and Boone went for a walk. False spring had entered Santa Fe. Warm winds blew up from the south, making the sea of mud worse than ever. Nevertheless, they were joyful as colts in a new-green pasture as they toured the city. Resa was especially happy. The previous night she had slept by Boone, her hands playing carefully over his skin. In her delight, she hadn't bothered to wear her nightdress, and she was embarrassed when Maria wakened them with hot coffee in the morning.

"You'll have to be moving back to the house, soon," said Boone as they crossed the street by the church. "You've already created a scandal."

"Who cares? I love you too much to worry what anyone thinks."

They rounded the corner of the church. Miss McShane, Resa's teacher, was coming down the street.

"Oh, Miss McCutcheon, Mr. Garcia. I was just on my way to deliver a message to you."

"What message?" Boone raised his eyebrows.

"Since Miss McCutcheon has been absent from school, and since she has been inhabiting your establishment, the parents of the school children insisted that I drop her from the roll," she mumbled, staring down at her mud-covered shoes.

"But, surely, Miss McShane, since Miss McCutcheon has been my nurse and hasn't had the run of the premises except for my room and the kitchen, a compromise can be reached."

"I'm afraid not. Mrs. Pryne insists. Otherwise she will remove me from my job. Resa's very bright. She should continue her education. Yet, I have no other means of support and I must make a living. Surely you understand."

"Mrs. Pryne again." Boone shook his head. "I'd like to confront her with Mr. Pryne's doings. It'd take her down a peg."

"If I drop school, may I still borrow books from you?" asked Resa.

"Surely," Miss McShane smiled kindly, then blushed.

"Then, it's settled."

"But, Resa—" Boone began to say.

"And I won't move back to the house, either. Maria and I will stay where we are. Who cares about the bluenoses of Santa Fe?"

"If you'll excuse me, then . . ." Miss McShane walked away. Her face was red as an apple at harvest.

"Resa, you can't stay at the house," Boone explained. "The girls have been patient with you and Maria while I've been ill, but you must understand their need for privacy."

"Why? What do they do that you and I don't?"

"It's not the same."

"Of course it is, only they get paid for it and they aren't lucky enough to have just one lover."

"Still, I'll have to insist that you move."

"Can I stay until day after tomorrow?"

"Sure." Boone hesitated, then said, "You know I'll miss you."

"Then let me stay," Resa pleaded. "Nobody'll dare say anything about it with you and Charlie."

"No!"

Resa was angry. She was confused at the feelings within her, the split between her love for Boone and his hateful way of living.

Boone tried to appease her, and asked, "In the spring, would you like to set up your shop?"

"Now that I'm out of school, it'll be fine." She chatted as they continued their walk, planning the shop. She was excited.

Yet even after she and Maria moved back to her place, Resa often came up the back steps of the house to visit Boone. She was lively as the false spring, as blustery with her plans as the spring winds that pummeled the town. Sometimes Boone was distracted, but she thought it was only his business worries, for with the thaw, his business was expanding.

One afternoon she rushed up the back stairs singing. In her hand was the freight bill for her first load of fabrics. She'd sell her mother's jewels to Boone now and get the cash for her shop.

She knocked on his door.

"It's me, Boone," she called impatiently.

"Just a minute." A muffled answer greeted her. She knew he was in bed. Sleep clogged his voice.

In a minute he opened the door a crack, a peculiar look on his face. "Go down to the kitchen and get me some coffee, will you? I just woke up."

She turned to go when she saw something move behind him. She craned her neck around his shoulder. In the bed, Gloria turned over, mumbling something as she reached for Boone's body.

Without saying a word, Resa turned and stalked to the kitchen. She got two cups of coffee from the cook and brought them back to Boone's room. When she walked in, loudly pushing the door with her foot, Gloria was nowhere to be seen.

"I brought coffee," she said spitefully. "One for you and one for your stinking whore!"

"Whore?" Boone feigned surprise.

"Don't lie to me, Boone Garcia! I saw her in your bed. That Gloria!"

"Resa, I . . ."

Without waiting for him to finish, she tossed the coffee on him. He yelped. Grabbing her, he threw her to the floor.

"Bitch!" he yelled, as he peeled his wet

clothes off.

"What did you think," Resa shouted from where she had collapsed on the floor, "that I'd go for the coffee all meek and mild while she had time to slink back to her corner?"

"You little hellcat!" He struggled out of his clothes. "For two bits, I'd beat you."

"Go ahead. It wouldn't hurt half as much as what you just did. I want my mother's jewels, *now!*"

Resa was so angry she was shaking, yet her voice told her she sounded deadly calm.

Boone didn't answer.

Resa rose to her feet and asked evenly, "How long you been sleeping with her?"

"That's none of your business," he answered coldly. "If you hadn't come nosing around here when you're not expected, you'd never have known."

"That's not what counts."

"Now don't go getting all moral on me, Resa."

"What about my mother's jewelry?" she demanded.

He was standing facing the desk, his back toward her. His stance was the picture of disdain.

"I don't have it," he finally said.

"What? Where is it?"

"I had to pay Becky's pimp off. He left

town. The jewels went for her." He paused. "Lately I've been losing."

Resa's world caved in on her. Gone was her trust in Boone. Gone was her independence.

"It'll only be a little while." He put on his dressing gown, which had been on the bed. "I'll pay you back, I promise."

"You sonofabitch," Resa hurled at him. "As to us, that's finished!"

"Something had to give," Boone answered calmly. He walked out the door, and left her clench-fisted to stare at his back.

"How could you sell my jewels for a whore?" she shouted in fury.

Boone laughed. "I told you, I am what I am." He went down the stairs.

She stood with her hands on her hips. She paced back and forth across the room as though jerked by invisible strings.

As Boone reached the last step, he heard Resa's voice, "If you want a whore, I'll show you a whore!" Her voice was calm as she stalked out the door.

That night as the wind howled outside and the temperature dropped, signaling the end of the false spring, Resa—made up to the hilt, wearing a low-cut black dress with bugle beads along the bust line, and with a black ostrich feather with jewels at the base poked in her hair—strode slowly down the staircase that led to the front parlor. Maria stood at the top of the stairs, fingering her rosary.

Gloria and Boone were already below, he at the poker table, she greeting three customers who'd just come off the trail and stank. The piano jangled. Men, some dressed in suits, some in buckskin, raised their eyes as Resa walked down the stairs.

"Hey, Gloria, who's the new filly?" someone called. "Resa," she replied. Boone raised his eyes to hers. He was thunderstruck. His eyes followed hers as she descended.

"Whooooeeee," one wrangler yelled. "Let me at her."

"She'll cost more than you've seen for a year, Lanie," Boone replied. "Let's play poker!" He shuffled the cards.

"Why's she so special?"

"She's new to the life," said Gloria as she crossed the room and extended her hand toward Resa. "Come, Resa, I've somebody for you," she said as she guided Resa toward a fat old man who sat in the corner, his pudgy fingers rubbing the top of his cane.

"Be good to Mr. Tracy, Resa. He's one've our best customers." Gloria left them. Resa had to fight the impulse to spit down the back of Gloria's peacock blue gown.

Chapter Ten

The winter hung on and on. For weeks Resa dreamed of nothing but men's privates; the smell of semen; the rankness of male sweat and tobacco-stinking spit; the odor of liquor floating up from the maws of the men. Their names were quickly forgotten, these men who assailed her night after night. Sometimes she awakened in a cold sweat. Always she feared that someone would beat her. She knew from the others that Charlie came to the rescue only when he sensed a girl legitimately feared for her life.

"I've become the worst of the worse," she said to Maria. "Nothing's keeping you here. Leave. Go back to your people."

"When I needed help, you hired me," Maria said tersely. "Kept the children. I'm staying."

"But I can't pay you."

"Gloria says I can be cook's helper, a maid. We go to church. *Nuestra Señora* help us now."

Maria closed up the house and moved to The Golden Web where she moved in with the cook in a tiny room in back of the kitchen.

Saturday afternoon, Maria came to Resa's room. Resa raised her eyes from a book. She hid in her books, never leaving her room when she could help it.

"We go to confession. You feel better," she said.

"I can't," Resa said listlessly.

"You want to go to hell?" Maria's eyes widened in fear.

"I'm already there." Yet Resa put down her book and followed Maria down the steps and, for the first time in weeks, out into the world.

She spent over an hour at her penance. Maria waited for her at the back of the church.

"I feel better than I have since my family died," she said, wiping her eyes, as they left the church.

That Sunday she went to church, sitting at the back. She got ice-pick stares from the congregation as she came down from the rail. It didn't bother her. Every Sunday she went to church. Every Sunday she had time to think as the others prayed.

"Don't it hurt like hell? Your back? It's black and blue," said Maria one night as she laced Resa into her black corset. She patted Resa's shoulder. She seemed near tears.

"This won't go on much longer," Resa whispered in pain.

"I could kill Garcia," Maria swore.

"Killing him won't help. Let me think some more."

Garcia had left Resa pretty much alone since the night she walked down the stairway for the first time. He was polite. Nothing more. One night he got a little drunk and, by mistake—he later claimed—

had stumbled into her room near dawn, rousing her from her whirling sleep.

"Resa, I . . ."

"You what? Working hours are over," she'd said stonily.

"I miss you, Resa."

She grabbed the heavy candlestick that sat on her nightstand.

"I'll use it."

"Taught you all you know, and you act like this," he smiled drunkenly.

"There are some things even a whore doesn't have to do."

"Bitch!" He turned and walked out, staggering against the door as he left. "I taught you good. You're the best girl in the place and that's the thanks I get for it."

She threw the candlestick behind him. It hit against the doorjamb with a thud. She was so angry she couldn't sleep the rest of the night, but she was proud. She realized that she truly hated him. She would do anything to get away, to take revenge on Garcia.

The following Saturday, after confession, Resa and Maria took a long walk through the muddy streets, up onto the bench behind Santa Fe.

"When you're cleaning, do you go into Mr. Garcia's office?" Resa asked her friend.

"No. He never lets me. Says he'll kill me if he catches me there."

"Do you clean his bedroom?"

"Yes. Clean sheets once a week, dusting twice a week."

"Tell me everything you know about everybody there. Strengths. Weaknesses. Who drinks. Who smokes opium. How they spend their time."

"Becky smokes opium. Gloria fined her half a week's pay last week. I heard them fighting about it."

"No wonder she's always so pale."

"Rita and Nita chew peyote, but only when Gloria's out of the house. Then they get sick and throw up.

"Martha and Red drink and drink when they're alone," Maria continued. "Gloria catches them, she fines them. When they're drunk, they sleep together. Sometimes when they're sober, too."

"Charlie?"

"He's like Garcia. He doesn't drink too much or use anything else besides his pipe, but he sure spends a lot of time with Becky. I think he uses his whole paycheck on her."

"It's easy for you to learn things. For me it's harder. The others treat me like I have two heads."

"You aren't like them. You read too

much. Mostly they're jealous you make so much money. Martha and Red were talking with Rita and Nita the other night. 'We should get her down and black both her eyes,' Martha said. 'That'd keep her from thinking she's some kind of religious saint.'

"'She's a prissy bitch,' said Red. 'I'd like to ram a hot poker up her ass.'

"'She took half my best callers,' said Rita.

"'Mine too,' said Nita. 'We should teach her a lesson.'

"That's when I dumped a platter of steaks right in Nita's lap. It was an awful thing, but it sure made me feel good."

Resa asked, "Was that the row when Gloria had to break everybody up?"

"Yeah. They was all over me, but I've had worse."

They both laughed.

"Dear Maria."

"You'll figure something out. You've got a way with people. Even Garcia. Sometimes he looks at you like he doesn't know what to make of you. Like he wants you back, but is scared of you, too."

"He can't own me," Resa said with determination. "Nobody can."

The next day the weather turned sunny. Gloria had the doors and windows opened. Maria took up the rugs and beat them outside. Resa hated the breeze that flapped through her room. The sunshine seemed too bright, a reminder that it would be easy to give in to the dark. *If I don't get out of here soon, I'll turn into just another whore. One who reads maybe, but just another whore nevertheless.* She forced herself out of bed and, in her gown, she stood near the window, looking out at the streets where wagons and carriages went by, where there was life. The street vendors were back. The Indians would be in front of the Palacio selling things. She ached to join them and stamped her foot in frustration. Then she made herself stretch and breathe deeply.

In the rush before the business hour, Maria ran excitedly into Resa's room. "When I took up the carpet in Garcia's room today," she whispered, "I found a hole in the floor. It looks down on his office."

Resa caught Maria by the hands, swung her around and jumped up and down.

"Maria, I could kiss you."

"Becky needs lacing."

"Thanks."

All evening, the wheels turned in her head. She was so distracted, two of her patrons accused her of being drunk. Thankfully, a young man, Jim Rolfson, who was heading back to his dad's ranch the next day did her the favor of buying the whole night, forking over his five dollars. He was seventeen and randy as a rooster. Jim was a handsome shiftless lad. After Resa took care of him she was free to think.

Jim snored. To the rhythm of his raucous blatting, Resa devised her plan.

"Maria, I need a new box of face powder. Will you get it for me from the store room?" Resa called that night.

When Maria arrived Resa closed the door behind them. "We must have a signal. I want to watch the office. If Garcia's there, he'll hear me if I walk on the floor above, so I must never be caught in his room.

"You spend most of your time on the ground floor. I'll start reading in the parlor instead of here. When your apron's tucked up into your waist, on this corner, like so, it'll mean he's gone out of that room. I'll go up to his bedroom and watch when he comes back in. When he goes out again, you call out. Ask if anybody wants something to drink. Then I can leave."

"Be careful, Little One." Though Maria wanted Resa to escape, she knew Garcia too well and worried for Resa's sake.

"I will. You be careful, too."

From his room, Resa watched Garcia's comings and goings. Garcia's bedroom and the office were the only rooms in the house with locks on the doors. When she went in to spy, she locked herself in his bedroom, so if anybody tried the door it would look as if Boone were there.

She learned that after the house closed, between three and four a.m., Garcia unlocked the office to bank the night's receipts. He carefully separated the pay into two stacks, one from the bar, one from the house. He kept meticulous books. Then he put the bar money in the safe by his desk. The rest—by far the larger stack—he stashed in a strongbox concealed behind thick volumes near the floor of the bookcase on the south wall. Always, he came to the desk when he was finished, poured himself two whiskeys, which he sipped slowly. It was his thinking time, when he sat puffed like an adder, admiring his enterprise.

In the afternoon he took money from the safe to the bank. Some days he paid the brewer or the baker or the laundryman. He allowed them in the office. Conspicuously he paid them from the safe.

Mondays Boone opened the strong box, took a small part of the money, and banked that, too.

By the pcephole, Resa glowed with amusement.

You're hoist on your own petard, Garcia. His suspicious nature was catching up with him.

Jim Rolfson was back in town that week. Resa flirted with him as though he were the apple of her eye. He was cute in his shiftless naiveté. He took to bringing her candy, which she shared with the girls.

"You're almost like a beau," she said to him between bites of molasses.

"Shucks, Resa. You're worth every penny. Gloria says we can spend the week together."

"How much did that cost you?"

"Fifty. My old man'll have a fit, but who gives a damn?" He grinned at her.

Sunday morning Resa got the signal from Maria that Boone was closing the bar.

"I've planned a lovely surprise for you," she said to Rolfson, steering him toward Rita and Nita. "I thought you'd like a change, so I've set it up with the twins to take care of you tonight." She handed him over to the giggling twins. In his tipsiness, he went without an argument. "They'll drop you back in my bed when they've finished with you."

"I love you," he called, as she went up the stairs. Nita and Rita laughed.

Resa locked herself in Garcia's room and drew back the rug over the peephole. He went through the routine. Everything was perfect, yet the strange feeling that hadn't haunted her since Badger came back was suddenly upon her. She had to fight not to run back to her room, to flee the sense of danger that assailed her. *I ignored you once. Damn near got beat to death for it. Not ever again.*

Yet the house was quiet. Boone sat, unmoving. *What* bothered her? At last Boone replaced the whiskey bottle and his glass at the edge of the desk. He stood up and blew out the lantern.

She gave him ten seconds to cross the room and lock the door. Quickly, she put the rug smoothly back in place and, unlocking the door from the inside, she entered the hall.

There, in the dim lantern light, was Charlie.

"What you doing in there, Resa?"

She jumped. That was the danger. Simultaneously, she heard Boone coming up the stairs.

"It's been an awful night," she invented quickly. "The worst—that puking drunk

151

from Taos, who heaved all over the bed, then that skunk who whipped me. Rolfson paid for my time, then Gloria doubled up on me when he got drunk. I . . . I just feel lonely for the good old days, I guess. I just went to see Boone's room. To remember what it was like once." She faked tears as she leaned against Charlie's shoulder.

"You giving Becky the night off?" Boone said as he approached them.

"Hell no," said Charlie. "Resa's just feeling down, that's all."

"Well, she'd better get some sleep or she'll miss church tomorrow."

He went into his room and locked the door behind him.

"Thanks for not telling him," Resa said to Charlie. "I'd rather die than have him know how much I miss him sometimes."

"It's all right."

"Night, Charlie."

Her heart was in her throat as she closed her door. *Soon. It's gotta be soon. Next week.* Her hands shook as she took off her robe and climbed over Rolfson's sleeping hulk to the other side of her bed.

Chapter Eleven

The following day, after church, Resa laid out her plan to Maria as they walked along the streets. Resa gave Maria every dime she had in the world except twenty dollars. Ducking into an alley, Maria shoved the money into her blouse where it nestled between her ample breasts.

"I'm going to miss you, Maria. Soon we'll

be out of this. Be careful." She and Maria split up as they walked to the house. Maria took the back entrance, while Resa entered at the front.

"If you hadn't been here in five minutes, I was sending Charlie out to look for you," barked Gloria.

"It was such a beautiful day. I guess I got caught up daydreaming," Resa lied.

"Well, you almost daydreamed away twenty-five dollars. Rolfson cleared out. Said he'll be back late in the week. Mr. Pryne came in half an hour ago. He's taking supper with us and he wants you."

"After all the trouble he's given Garcia, he's got his nerve," Resa griped.

"A customer's a customer. Treat him right."

"I'd like to treat him with red pepper on his balls."

"Shut up!" Yet Gloria was amused. She laughed as she walked with Resa to the table. "You just may make it yet, kid," she said.

Tuesday Martha complained that somebody had stolen her best black crepe with its high neck and buttons. Maria and Gloria combed all the girls' wardrobes for it but came up empty-handed. "I don't know why you think one of the others took it," said

Gloria. "It's too huge for anybody else to get any good of it."

"Maybe one of your admirers took it to play with," said Nita.

"It'd fit most men," said Gloria. "Maybe we've a caller with a fancy for black crepe."

Wednesday, Maria went off to buy vegetables at the market. That night she whispered to Resa, "I got everything you need. It's in an east corner of the stable under some feed sacks." Then she shoved something into Resa's hand. Resa took the tiny vial. She put it between the pages of *Don Juan*. The other girls might riffle her underwear or look through her clothes, but she knew they wouldn't fool with a book.

Thursday night was one of the busiest in Resa's experience. Spring weather was bringing crowds out. Several wagon trains had hit town that week, along with several herds of cattle and the punchers that went with them. From Fort Union, a company of men came in on leave. They were tired of chasing Comanches, and wanted a more citified diversion than the fandango halls of Loma Parda, where they could get all the services, but not the comforts of The Golden Web.

There were fights between the wranglers and the soldiers. The bar got busted up before Charlie, with an assist from the sheriff, hauled the worst offenders off to the jail. The melee started when the soldiers demanded that they be serviced in a group, and the wranglers weren't ready to wait.

Resa was tired, but Martha and Red had an argument that lasted past dawn. They pulled one another's hair and threw things. Even after Charlie threatened to take them to jail, and Gloria fined them their night's take, they kept it up past six a.m.

Friday night Resa came down to dinner, dressed in her usual black.

"Where's Maria?" she asked casually when the other cook grouchily served her.

"She quit. One of her relatives is sick. Dumb Indian. She leaves me alone with the weekend coming, with all the stayovers. Crap!"

God keep you safe, Maria. She ate in silence, scarcely paying attention to the others.

That night Rolfson was back. To prove she'd learned it all, Resa tried every trick she knew on him.

"Golly. You sure give a guy his money's worth," he said as he lay by her in the early morning. "You ever thought about giving this up? Settling down?"

"Rely on a man? Never." She smiled at

the boy.

"Well, if you ever change your mind, let me be the first to know."

"That's sweet, but your Dad would skin you if he heard you talk that way to the likes of me."

"What's he got to do with it?"

"Plenty. He'd run you off if you ever married a 'soiled dove.' You've had it too easy. You can't make it without the Rolfson purse."

"Aw, Resa. It's not true. I could set up a spread of my own. We'd do fine together."

"Maybe you would. I'm not cut out to work myself to death on some ranch—scratching my fingers to the bone, having a baby every year. It's just not my style."

She ran her fingers through his hair, massaged the muscles of his neck. Soon he was asleep. She reviewed everything again. There was only one hard spot. She *had* to make Boone let her into the office.

After work Sunday morning, Resa went downstairs with her last caller and waved him goodbye as he mounted up.

"You're friendly tonight," said Gloria as she locked the door.

"Have you seen Garcia?"

"He's in the office. Why?"

"I want to talk to him."

"Well, you can wait for him if you like. I'm going to bed. What a night." She went up the stairs.

Momentarily Resa waited to be certain Gloria had gone in her room. She collected herself. The vial pressed against her breast like a hot iron. In the parlor, by herself, she shook her arms and legs, forcing herself to relax. Then she strode casually to the office door and knocked timidly.

"Who is it?"

"It's Resa. I want to talk to you."

"Just a minute, Resa. I'll be right out."

"No. I want to come in. This is confidential."

"All right. Just a minute."

She could see him in her mind's eye, checking to see that the books were even in the bookcase, that the ledgers were carefully closed, that the safe door was shut.

Finally, he opened the door. The windowless office smelled musty of cigars, money, and brandy.

"I've been screwing up my courage to talk to you," Resa said shyly, shutting the door behind her.

"Courage isn't all you've been screwing." He sat behind the desk, coolly assessing the woman she had become.

"I've decided this place is too small.

There's a perfect building on the outskirts of town; you know, out by that blacksmith shop up the hill."

"I know the place. Go on."

"I'm sick and tired of being banged. I want to open a house, but I need your permission and your backing. If you pay to have it renovated and if you put in the fixtures, I can recruit the girls and we'll both make out fine."

"You know what you're letting yourself in for?" Boone asked measuredly.

"I've watched Gloria. There's nothing she can do that I can't, only I won't make so many enemies. I won't let my girls get started on drinking and dope. That way they'll last longer."

"I'll take forty per cent off the top the first year, twenty after that."

"Fine. We'll make good money. I'll be off my backside."

Boone laughed. "I always knew you had it in you." He came from behind the desk and held her.

"Oh, Boone." She closed her eyes and kissed him full on the mouth, a burning hunger within her overpowering her business sense.

"God in heaven, I've missed you," she said. He was stroking her arms, about to run his fingers down her dress, when she said, "Oh!" and fell into a dead faint in his arms.

He lay her gently on the floor, staring uncomfortably around for something to revive her. Then he left the room to get some water.

The instant he was out the door, heading for the kitchen Resa jumped up and dropped the knockout drops from the vial into the bottle on his desk. Then she rearranged herself exactly as she'd been when she fainted.

Boone came in with a towel and glass of water. He bent over her slapping her wrists, dabbing at her forehead and cheeks uncomfortably, trying to get the water to her lips.

Soon she revived. "Too much excitement," she mumbled as he rubbed her hands, then gently drew her to him.

"Too much Saturday night," he said. He kissed her again. He took her hair down, dropping her feathers to the floor. "It could be good with us again. Gloria never meant anything to me."

"Can we talk about it tomorrow?" she said in a small voice. "I'm shaky. Better get some rest."

"You want help up the stairs?"

"No. But don't forget what I was asking you." She smiled. "Part of me will always love you, Boone."

Slowly she walked up the steps, yet her mind was racing ahead. She went to her room, made a show of closing the door loudly enough that, if he were listening, he'd know she was in her room. She fumbled by candlelight, for her jewelry box. She pulled down the top of her dress and pinned the amythyst pin to her camisole, wondering at her sentimentality. She sat on the bed slowly counting to two hundred. The house was as quiet as it ever got. From one of the rooms, a loud snore of a stayover escaped into the hall. She smelled it again— the tobacco, stale booze, soap, disinfectant. Faintly, under those odors lingered the last remnants of burnt wood from fires in months past.

When she was through counting, she walked quietly to her door, let herself out, and tiptoed down the hall to Boone's room. She was relying on his habit of those two whiskeys. She knew that if something prevented him from drinking, the jig was up.

In his room, she cautiously drew back the rug. In the lantern light below, she saw Boone's figure slumped over the desk.

Like a cat fleeing a pack of dogs she was down the stairs. She stopped at the storage

161

room and pulled off one of the dark shelves a huge carpet bag Maria had concealed there earlier in the week. She went into the office. She checked to be certain Boone was unconscious. Then she removed the keys from his pants, unfastening the chain clasped to his belt loop. She removed the books that hid the strongbox. She took the strongbox out. It was very heavy. Resa fumbled with the keys until she found the one that fit.

She stuffed the money and some papers from the box into the carpet bag. On the way out, just to be certain, she checked the safe, but it was locked.

"Goodbye, you bastard," she mumbled as she looked back at Boone one last time.

She rushed silently to the kitchen, lugging the heavy carpet bag, and unlocking the door, she went to the stable at the back. She took the keys with her, hoping to cause Boone even greater inconvenience and embarrassment when everybody in the house learned how he had been tricked.

In the stable, under a pile of feed sacks, was an assortment of things that Maria had secreted there. Boone's black and white pinto whinnied in recognition as she entered.

"Shut up," she hissed at him.

Her ears were listening constantly for the arrival of Maria. She had almost finished dressing when she heard horses approaching.

Maria reined up by the stable. Quickly she dismounted and helped Resa load the money from the carpet bag into saddlebags. Then she helped Resa mount the sidesaddled horse that she'd led in.

"*Jesus, Maria.* There's lots here," she breathed.

"You look silly as a *torero* with his pants slit," she softly giggled.

"Let's get!" Maria whispered, and spurred her horse forward and away from The Golden Web.

The women rode out into the faint gray of the dewy dawn. Anyone watching them riding through the almost deserted streets saw a fat old woman, dressed in mourning, for Resa had taken Martha's dress and stuffed pillows and padding into it until she looked even bulkier than the old prostitute herself. She rode sidesaddle and looked like a whale astride. Her face and hair were covered with a heavy mourning veil. Maria, dressed like a man, rode behind her, with her saddlebags filled.

By the time they reached Santa Domingo pueblo, Maria's home, it was early morning. They stopped only long enough on the trail for Resa to remove the crazy clothes she wore out of town, to change into men's clothes.

"It's a good thing the missionary's sister let me borrow that sidesaddle. It really completed the disguise," laughed Maria.

"I hate it. Can't wait to get a regular one."

In the pueblo, women were stirring outside fires to fire pottery. Dogs lay in the June sunshine or trotted about their errands. Children ran in the sandy streets, chasing a ball with sticks. Some men, on the pueblo's outskirts, tended small fields of corn.

"What will they think of an Anglo hiding here?"

"Everybody knows you're invisible."

They dismounted and put their horses in a corral to the west of the pueblo. Trying not to create any attention, they walked down the pueblo's back street. Soon they were inside the second floor of an adobe building.

Maria introduced Resa to her sister and mother. The five children who had stayed for a few days at Resa's house smiled shyly at her. Their smiles filled the tiny white-washed room with its dirt-packed clean floor. Maria's sister set steaming plates of tortillas and menudo before them; she shoved the children out to play.

"It's not as nice as the house or La Fonda," apologized Maria.

"It's the best home I've had for years."

The women, who spoke little English, smiled at the tone of her voice. They were mending.

Soon Resa and Maria found some sheepskin blankets. Birdsongs and children's voices were their lullaby.

Resa awoke to the odor of mutton stew, smiling to herself as she pictured Boone Garcia, who was probably back on his feet by now, rushing around Santa Fe searching for his treasure.

A few days will tell the story. Before I can begin to feel free. "What's cooking?" she said to Maria, who was helping the women mend. "I'm starved."

Chapter Twelve

Resa's imagined picture of Garcia wasn't far from wrong. Just as she figured, he and Charlie combed Santa Fe high and low looking for her.

"She dropped off the earth. Her horse is still in the stall. She didn't take the stage. Nobody saw her. Where the hell's the bitch disappeared to?" Garcia's head pounded.

"Either she's hiding here or she's had help getting out of town," said Charlie.

"See if you can find anybody who has seen her. I'll talk to the girls."

Rita quickly came up with the recollection that Resa had told her about Jim Rolfson's offer of marriage.

"She'd never have told Rita she was going away with Rolfson if she planned on it," Boone figured. "It stinks, but if we don't find her in town by tomorrow, Charlie, we'd better ride out to Rolfsons and see."

"Jim Rolfson's a nice kid, but everybody knows he's kinda shiftless. If he and Resa planned to run off together, maybe she took the money to set him up. His old man would never give him a stake if he knew Jim had taken up with Resa. The Rolfsons are too dignified."

"Maybe she did take the money for him," Boone sighed. "But I doubt it."

For two days they combed Santa Fe with carding boards, but they didn't find a trace of Resa. On the third day, Boone and Charlie began the long ride to Rolfson's. Yet something pricked at Boone and he called a halt.

"I think I heard her say once that Maria's from Santa Domingo. She suckered me once. I'll be damned if I'll let her sucker me

167

again. I'll bet she went there. And so help me God, if I catch her, I'll flay her alive!''

"You go to Santa Domingo, I'll continue to Rolfson's," said Charlie. "That way we've got both bets covered. If you find her you'll have the pleasure of kicking in her teeth."

"If you find her, bring her back. Tie her to the horse. I'll deal with her."

They split up, Charlie riding north, Garcia south. The longer Garcia rode the more time he had to think of ways he'd finish off Resa McCutcheon.

Yet at Santa Domingo no one claimed to have seen either Maria or an Anglo woman.

As he rode out of the pueblo, back toward Santa Fe, his sense told him he'd been lied to. He knew Resa was either there or had been there. The hairs that rose on his neck as he walked the pueblo's streets confirmed it. He was angry, frustrated. He pounded leather, tiring the pinto until he finally got off and walked him, knowing if he didn't he'd run him into the ground.

Back in Santa Fe, Charlie told Garcia, "Jim Rolfson was at the main ranch when I rode in. Claimed he never saw Resa after that last Friday night. I believe him. He was real sad to hear she was gone."

"She's done it!" Garcia raged. "Damn

her, she's done it! There was plenty money she took. But, more important, the damn-fool kid got maybe sixty thou in mining stock certificates from Virginia City. It was my getting-out money."

Ol' Garcia's been had. Serves him right and good luck to you Resa, Charlie thought as he went to see Becky.

Part Two

Chapter Thirteen

The freight wagon stood at Devil's Gate toll road in Gold Canyon. It was laden to the brim. Next to the driver, Resa and Maria were wedged tightly in the seat.

"Hornaday! What you doing freighting women? Hell, I've never seen you look so sober."

The gateman reached in his back pocket,

drew out a bottle and handed it up to the driver. Behind the wagon, a line of wagons was building up.

"He's not drinking," said Resa. She took the change the driver handed her. The driver shook his head at the offer of whiskey. "Crazy women! I smashed jug already at Sacramento. Catch you on the way back."

The gatekeeper whooped and threw his hat into the crisp air. "Never thought I'd see the day somebody'd get you sober for a run."

"It'll be the last time," Hornaday called as he cracked his bull whip over the heads of the already-lathered mules in his six-up.

"I hate to destroy your reputation. But nothing's getting in the way of this load seeing Virginia City in one piece," said Resa.

Up the steep grade, the wagon struggled. In front of them a herd of cattle—maybe fifty—driven by three men, blocked the road. To the sides of them the canyon walls closed in. The load creaked along the deep, dusty ruts.

"Four more miles, ladies," Hornaday said. "But what a four miles. Damn steers. It'll take the rest of the day," he laughed. "Wait'll you see Virginia. Ugliest place this side of hell. What makes you think you'll pretty up the ladies there's beyond me. Hell, the wind'll blow you and your hats to kingdom come, come October."

"With the money here, a lady can have a hat a day. Who cares if one blows away?" Resa said.

"What's that?" Maria pointed to a huge building on the left, surrounded by small shacks. A network of trestles slid down the steep hills, over the building, where small cars ran.

"It's a mine. That's the hoist house on top. Down below's the mill." At that moment a steam whistle let loose its haunting cry. Up and down the canyon, other whistles shrilled. The mules jumped in their traces. Maria and Resa covered their ears. In front of them some of the herd bolted off the road into a dusty thicket of stunted willows. The wranglers dove into the thicket after the strays.

"Shift's changing," yelled Hornaday.

At the mine, men scurried out of the shacks surrounding it. They wore hats and pants, but no shirts. Some carried picks. They entered the hoist house.

Out of hoist house a stream of men poured. Some stopped to talk with the men going in, others walked straight ahead, the slouch of their shoulders proclaiming them too tired for amenities. Resa eyed one man in particular, a lank redhead whose pale skin was a dusty gray. He strode to his cabin, where a woman, who had been taking down a gray wash from a clothesline picked up her basket and joined him. They walked into their tiny shack. No tree. No grass. Not a flower was to be seen on the slope.

"A miner's wife?" she yelled to Hornaday over the bawling of the cattle.

"Yes. He's lucky. Most are single. I keep telling you, no woman in her right mind lives here unless she's a lady of the evening."

To their right, down near the base of the canyon, several Chinese in basket hats with blue clothes worked with picks, their queues sliding down their backs. Another Chinaman passed among them with buckets slung from his shoulders on a pole from which the men dipped a liquid. He chanted to them in a singsong language that Resa recognized from their brief stay in San Francisco.

"They work the dump," said Hornaday. "White miners hate them—worse than sin."

They entered Gold Hill. All traffic ceased as the cattle passed through the town. Wagons from the steep sidestreets, bearing ore, stood clogged in a jam with horses and carriages. In front of the saloons and the general store people waited for the herd to pass. Behind their wagon there was a line of wagons, horses and riders, a buckboard and a shay.

The mines ran into the town, dwarfing the shacks of the miners, dwarfing the Victorian mansions of the fortunate, which sat behind the stores and saloons, between the stores and saloons. Everything man-made except the mines, the dumps and the trestles, was dwarfed to insignificance.

Except the wind. In the heat, dust blew in eddies, then in face-scraping whirlwinds. They were at the bottom of a funnel, with the Washoe winds blowing down the canyon, threatening to sail man, beast, lumber and ore to the flatlands along the Carson River.

"Are you sure you wouldn't rather have stayed in San Francisco?" Resa yelled to Maria.

Maria didn't answer. The gusts were too strong. But she pointed to a nearby store, where five or six Indians squatted on the boardwalk playing dice against a wall. For the first time since they left Santa Domingo—catching the stage south through the Gila—she smiled a smile broad enough to show her gap-toothed happiness.

"Consarned, goldanged wind!" Hornaday drew his neckerchief under his eyes.

"Consarned, goldanged herd!"

Still they inched forward. Up. Up. Past more houses, a livery stable, a blacksmith shop.

Resa pulled on Hornaday's sleeve. "What's the building there?"

Hornaday's laugh was muffled by his neckerchief. "A two-story outhouse, missy. Snow gets twenty feet high."

It was her last comment before they reached Virginia City. The wind increased until she and Maria clung to the seats, eyes closed against the blasts on the bends that made the hills of San Francisco look tame.

As they rounded the last hairpin turn separating Virginia City and Gold Hill, Resa opened her eyes. She gazed to the South. Mountains, blue as turquoise in the distance, radiant through the dust, confined mostly to the canyon base, gave her a feeling of exhilaration.

The wagon lurched forward. She heard shouts. She watched the buckaroos herd the cattle off to the right. At the crest of a nearby hill, she smelled what could only be a slaughterhouse. Its corrals were filled with bawling beasts, waiting their turns to fill miners' plates.

"Thank God they're off this road!" shouted Hornaday.

"Yah. Such dirt." Maria beat her sleeves and smoothed her skirt.

"Burned one load of clothes when we got to San Francisco. We'll burn another to-night," Resa said. "I could bathe for a week."

"I'll wash my hair. Seems like a year since we left Santa Fe," said Maria.

"Only three months." Resa turned to Hornaday. "Take us to the best hotel in town."

"That'll be the Sharon. What're you gonna do with the load?"

"I'll rent a room for it. 'Til I get settled."

Hornaday shrugged. Everything about these women was queer. Why should he argue with a fact?

Virginia City spread around them. It was an extension of Gold Hill, sloping the other way down the east face of Mount Davidson.

They drove past a row of saloons and shops, past lawyers' offices, past The Wells Fargo, past banks. Everywhere throngs milled along the streets, oblivious to the wind that swayed the wooden arcades fronting the buildings, covering board-walks, of streets unimaginatively named C and D.

On the left she saw a fine three-story building with the sign, "Sharon House."

"I'll never find space to unload here," Hornaday grumbled. "Sure you won't let me take this stuff to a warehouse?"

"It stays with me, Hornaday. I'll rent the rooms. You scout around for somebody to help us. Tell them I'll pay top dollar."

She and Maria climbed stiffly down from the wagon. Hornaday let fly a stream of tobacco juice, narrowly missing Resa's filthy skirt, before he turned the wagon down a side street, so steep it seemed to vanish.

They entered the Sharon House. The desk clerk, accustomed as he was to seeing strange people, raised his eyebrows at the couple approaching the desk. The young woman, dressed in battered riding skirt and a soiled blouse stank to high heaven as did the Indian who accompanied her. The Indian carried two carpetbags; the young woman—a girl, really—hefted a Sharps that was almost as big as she was. In the moment before the girl slapped one hundred dollars in gold coins onto the counter, he was considering asking his bouncer to send them, bag and baggage, to the street.

"I hear this is the fanciest place in town," Resa said.

"Sharon House has that reputation."

"Fine. I want two adjoining rooms, one

180

for my goods, one for my friend and me. I want the hottest bath this side of Hell. I want a big breakfast—steak and eggs—for two. And bring champagne and coffee. Does this hotel have a vault?"

"Yes."

"Is it watched?"

"Of course."

"Then I want this deposited."

Maria dragged the saddlebags onto the counter. Resa stood warily by, her hand ready to draw.

Resa made stack after stack of gold coins, in neat piles, before the clerk. His mind jumped ahead of him, as she counted in silence. He'd seen silver bars and gold dust. Yet never in the hands of a girl had he seen so much money. When the bags were almost empty except for the stock certificates and their few extra clothes, Resa closed them.

"I'll want a receipt," she said curtly.

"But, surely a bank . . ."

"The receipt, please."

The clerk called for help. His assistant put the coins in the vault, while Resa waited for her receipt.

"Can I see the vault? . . . I just have to be sure."

"Follow me." The clerk didn't like the girl's companion. She looked dangerous.

He opened the gate behind the counter. The girl walked with him to the room behind the counter where the vault stood. She seemed satisfied, and tipped him five dollars.

"Now don't forget: bath, champagne and breakfast."

"Certainly, young lady." He motioned the bellboy to take her bags.

The bellboy looked ridiculous carrying two empty carpetbags up the stairs.

Hornaday entered the lobby with three men.

"Got help," he called.

"I'll be right down, Hornaday," Resa answered. "Start carrying everything up to Room 212. I'll be right there with the key."

She and Maria stopped long enough to notice that the room was fine. Not as nice as the Lick Hotel in San Francisco, but better than they'd expected.

"I'm glad you decided to come here," said Maria.

"You were wasting away in the city, Maria. Here we'll both find what we need. I didn't care much for the fog there, but it was sure pretty compared to this. At any rate, it was good to go there. Now I know where to buy merchandise." She put her hand on Maria's shoulder. "Come. If they break one thing, I'll have Hornaday's head."

She encountered the men, coming up the stairs with boxes. She opened the room for them. "Just put them anywhere, but be careful."

Down on the street, people gathered in front of the Sharon House to watch. The wagon cover was pulled back, revealing an assortment of goods: boxes, Persian rugs, a sewing machine, two oak and glass display cases, a brass hall-tree and more boxes.

The clerk rushed out to the boardwalk and stood by Resa.

"Here, here. I'm not certain the management . . ."

"I'm paying for the room," she reminded him. "I'll pay extra if that's what it takes. It'll only be for a week or so. I won't leave my things in any filthy warehouse. Hold the bath and the food until I tell you." He went back inside.

"Yes, sir," Resa announced to the crowd. "In these boxes is the finest millinery east of San Francisco. Lots of it's from France. Gents, tell your ladies Mrs. Stafford Cluvier will be open for business as soon as I can find a suitable shop."

She and Maria helped the men unload. Evening darkened the streets by the time they were finished. She paid the men well, giving Hornaday two extra dollars. "For the bottle I broke," she said. "No hard feelings?"

"Well, I'll be damned. You're a Christian woman after all. It's been a pleasure, missy," he said. He waved goodbye to her and mounted the wagon to take the tired mules to their stable.

"Now you can order the bath and breakfast," Resa called to the clerk as she and Maria ascended the stairs.

Their room was more elegant than she at first thought. Its high ceilings had gas chandeliers. There was a sitting room and two large, brass beds.

The women stripped to the waist as they attacked the basin. Soon they had all their clothes off. They rummaged through their luggage and found robes.

Maria bounced and jounced on the snow white coverlet of the bed. *"Madre Maria,* it feels good," she proclaimed.

Soon the chambermaids brought in their baths. Resa and Maria rubbed scented soap over themselves.

"I'm *never* wearing these clothes again," Resa decided. She rang for the maid and had the clothes taken for burning. She did her hair, braiding it in a luxuriant chestnut queue.

"I'm going to get my hair dyed tomorrow. I'll fancy it black."

"Like an Indian's?"

"No. Like a rich Louisiana widow. From now on, I'm Mrs. Stafford Cluvier, a widow of a Confederate officer who died of a fever on the way West. You've become my friend through my trials on the trail. I met you in Denver. We went to San Francisco to buy our goods, and have come here to set up shop."

"You'll need a wedding ring."

"Tomorrow. But you'll have to buy it for me so nobody knows," Resa said conspiratorially. "And," she added, "Sunday we're going to church."

"After so long, Jesus will not know us."

"Pshaw, Maria."

Breakfast came. The waiter pretended nothing was out of the ordinary as he served two women with soaked hair, dressed like soiled doves, but acting like ladies, even if one was an Indian with three missing front teeth.

"I've never felt so free," said Resa when he left. "Money *is* freedom."

"Eat up. You're running off at the mouth like Nita."

Resa poured champagne.

"Mother and Father had champagne at

Christmas. Here's to Christmas in September in Virginia City—ugliest place a woman ever hoped to get pretty in." She raised her glass. Maria followed suit.

"It's awful," Maria grimaced. "I don't see why you like it."

"I don't. It's just to celebrate. We don't have to finish it."

After breakfast, they carefully unpacked their bags, stowing their bountiful San Francisco clothes in the dressers and in the wardrobe.

"I'll never wear pants again! I'll never wear black again," Resa chanted as she hung the clothes. "We spent like money was water, didn't we? Well, that's over. Now we get to be respectable."

"I'd rather ride all day than worry over clothes," said Maria.

Resa tucked her dainty black leather shoes next to Maria's bear-paw ones. Maria eyed her.

"You wasted your money on my shoes. Soon as I find some of my people, I'm going back to moccasins." She drew back the bedcovers and jounced onto the bed.

"Rich! I'm rich now," Resa exulted. "If I keep my head, I'm going to be richer."

Maria's reply was a snore.

Chapter Fourteen

Yet, in dawn's early light, as Resa looked out over the belching smokestacks of Virginia City from her window, the ebullience of the night before gave way to gray self-doubt.

That Saturday they walked from one end of the city to the other. There was no plan to the young metropolis. Mansions pushed proudly out of the B Street rocks, interspersed with livery stables and shacks. Below the saloons and businesses of C Street, appended to the backsides of the saloons, were the cribs and parlor houses of D Street, which gave way on the north and south to miners' shacks. Down the hill and to either end of D Street began the mines—their hoist houses crowded together, leaving spaces for gigantic piles of timbers, for the dumps that poked up everywhere, for the trestles that carried ore down to the mills, for the powder houses, and the monstrous storage bins under which a stream of mule-drawn ore wagons passed, gobbling up the ore from tipples, carrying it past the hospital down Six Mile Canyon to still other mills. There were breweries, bakeries, blacksmith shops—all thrown hastily together.

Except for a large truck garden near Chinatown, and for a few straggly lilac bushes and hollyhocks—long out of bloom—there was not a blade of grass or a tree in the whole dust-choked, windblown area. Some lonely Chinese Elms grew over the sand mounds in the cemetery to the north and east of the town.

"Those trees are so pretty, I'd almost die to be near one," Resa said. Maria grew more and more glum with each inch of the survey.

"I thought this would be better than San Francisco," Maria remarked. "It's wilder, but not wild enough."

Still, Maria's day wasn't wasted, for below the hospital she spied a nest of hovels where some Indians lived. Resa waited for her while she fairly ran to the shacks heaving stones at a pack of growling dogs around the doorway. She knocked on the first door and went inside. The dogs turned their attention to Resa, who was arming herself against their approach with stones, when a huge yellow cat strolled arrogantly by, teasing the dogs to chase her. She lured them under the overhanging rusted roof of a shed where another equally yellow, equally arrogant cat jumped on the back of one dog and rode him down the alley while others gave chase, barking, slavering to tear their enemy to pieces, ignoring the first cat who had ducked into a crevice by the shack. Just as a second dog was about to climb on the huge black and white victim of the feline circus ride, the cat jumped off and clawed its way through a tiny hole in the boards of a porch.

Maria came out of the shack. In her hands she carried her shoes. On her feet were moccasins.

"They're not like my people. They dress

189

like Anglos, talk like Anglos. For certain, they drink like Anglos. Everything there is dirty. The woman was drunk. They've come to Six Mile to work in the mills, but no one will hire them. They were run off their range last summer by a man who bought their land for a ranch. They don't want to go to the reservation, but they'll have to go soon."

"You must feel as hateful about Anglos as I felt about Yankees," Resa said thoughtfully.

Maria shrugged her shoulders. "Things change."

Still, for the rest of their tour, Maria was distracted. Resa knew she was thinking about the people in the shacks.

On the main street a woman walked by in the crowd wearing a mink cape, holding a brace of Afghan hounds on silver leashes, while her escort, a gambler, guided her by the arm. An organ grinder entertained on the corner across from the Sharon House. Children ran in and out of the crowds, some delivering packages, some chasing hoops.

They stared through the curtained window of a photography shop where three miners, dressed in black suits, waited, twirling their hats in their hands, to have their picture taken. Down a side street there was a pet store full of kittens and puppies, a parrot, and some monkeys. Resa hated the monkeys. They were too much like humans, eerie in their resemblance.

Next to the pet store was a saloon called the Last Chance. Next to it was a small shop with a "To Let" sign in the window. Next door was a bakery, where the clerk gave her the name of Baxter Thistle.

"He's a sharp one," said the baker, as Resa and Maria filled up with freshly baked raisin cookies.

"Don't let him overcharge you."

Brushing cookie crumbs off their faces, they went outside and leaned against the building.

"I'd rather fight off a whole house of men than do business with a stranger," Resa said.

"I'll protect you," said Maria, but she didn't sound very certain.

"Don't worry. I've an idea."

The next day she and Maria attended Mass at St. Mary's in the Mountains, the opulently furnished church which was the only building in Virginia City that competed with the mines in size.

"The church and the mines are equally impressive, one's steeple pushes toward God, the others' shafts dig down to the

191

Devil," Resa whispered as she eyed the tapestries on the walls and noticed the blue and red of the stained glass windows.

"There's no doubt which one's ahead," Maria said drily. Maria's head was throbbing from the noise of the saloons which had kept her awake most of the night.

In Resa's handbag were the stock certificates and a generous contribution.

"Fine to sit in front again." Resa nudged Maria as the choir entered.

After the service, they held back until the congregation filed out.

"I could see everything—the embroidery on the priest's stole, the flowers, everything. It's so fancy. The size of those candlesticks. In silver. Amazing," said Maria.

"I haven't met you before. I'm Fr. Bernard." The priest's complexion and hair claimed him for an Irishman. He extended his hand to them both.

"I'm Mrs. Stafford Cluvier. This is my friend, Maria Sanchez. We've come here under trying circumstances, Father. I need your help."

"Certainly."

"My husband, Colonel Stafford Cluvier, died outside Salt Lake City. We were coming west from New Orleans to San Francisco. Now I'm alone. My family died in the war. Maria and I went to San Francisco. It's too large. Too lonely. So I bought goods there, and plan to open a millinery, but I've no one to trust nor to protect my interests."

"What interests are those?"

"May we talk in private?"

He escorted them to his study at the base of the church and closed the door. Maria waited outside.

"My husband gave me these before he died. He told me to find good hands to put them in, but I don't know where to turn. I need a good business adviser."

She handed Fr. Bernard the stock certificates—shares in the Yellow Jacket, in the Imperial, in the California, in the Bullion. Five thousand shares in all.

He whistled.

"I'm not an authority on finances, mind you, but most of these are worth a lot. No wonder you want help.

"In the congregation are two men, Augustus and Claude Colbert. Augustus is Claude's father. They're a fine family. I've known them since I came here in '62. I watched Claude grow up. Augustus is a lawyer who deals in stocks. Claude just finished school—back east, somewhere, as a mining engineer.

193

"I blather on . . . anyhow, I'd recommend Augustus to you for his integrity."

"Wonderful. Will you please give me his address, and a letter of introduction?"

"Certainly." He reached for paper and pen. The office was as elaborately furnished as the church. As Fr. Bernard wrote, Resa noticed a wardrobe full of immensely valuable chasubles, many embroidered heavily with silver threads. The desk was mahogany. The walls were covered with fine religious paintings—originals—of scenes from the life of Christ. An immense silver crucifix hung behind Fr. Bernard. It was three feet long. The agony of Jesus gleamed through the room.

"I want some masses said for my husband's repose. Will two hundred dollars be enough for six months?"

"Indeed. I'll put him on my list immediately." Fr. Bernard drew a match from a silver holder on his desk. He lit some sealing wax, dropped it on the envelope, and pushed his ring into it.

"I know Stafford's with our Heavenly Father, but I hated so to leave him on the desert." Resa wiped her eyes daintily with her lace handkerchief. She rose.

"Here's the letter. I trust we'll be seeing you next Sunday." Fr. Bernard rose and shook her hand.

"Of course. I want a spiritual home in this awful place."

"I hate to lie to a priest." Resa joined Maria outside the study, where she was watching a drunk teeter down the hill, bottle in hand, toward a row of shacks.

"The money made up for your lie. Next time have masses said for *your* soul."

On Monday morning Resa pushed through the crowd of miners heading toward work on South C Street. She had dressed carefully, picking the most businesslike attire she could conceive—a dark gray skirt and jacket with a gray cape. Her bonnet was dark blue felt with a modest brim. Nevertheless, by the homage she received, she hadn't felt more naked as a whore. The miners, unaccustomed to seeing young women, bowed and tipped their hats. Resa blushed.

At Colbert, Attorney At Law, she felt dwarfed by the massive wainscoting of the outer office, by the huge leather chair into which she sank as the secretary, a dull-eyed young man with thick glasses, went to announce her.

Soon he returned, motioning her to follow.

Everything about the inner office made

her feel small—the arched windows facing the mine offices across the street, the highly-polished wood floors, the dark, green plaid paper on the walls, the immense mahogany desk with its ornate brass lamp, throwing a pool of golden light onto the dark green blotter, the bar at the left of the desk where there stood more bottles than she had seen at The Golden Web. Paintings of dark harvest scenes covered the walls. Resa thought of the journey from San Francisco and was amazed that such luxury could have been brought up these hills from whatever distance. She wanted to fade into the floor, yet she forced herself to be casual and, as the head behind the desk didn't immediately look up, she began strolling along the walls eyeing the pictures.

"Mrs. Cluvier?"

She unfastened her kid gloves. The left one pulled against the wedding band she had gotten a few days earlier, reminding her of her sham. She extended her hand.

"Mr. Colbert?"

"I've been reading Fr. Bernard's letter. Allow me to extend my condolences."

"Thank you. Can you help me?"

"What do you need?"

Augustus Colbert was short. Portly. With a broad smile and white hair. His hand lingered on hers. She fought the temptation to pull away.

"A woman alone must be very careful," Resa began.

"That's true."

"I have some money—about five thousand dollars. In addition, I have these."

She handed him the certificates. He took them and read through them, figuring on a tablet in front of him as he went. Resa was frightened. She felt that he would know she had forged the signatures on them, writing "Stafford Cluvier" in what she hoped was a masculine hand beneath "Boone Garcia."

"These, if traded, will bring you a considerable amount."

"How much?"

"Probably between eighty and eighty-five thousand dollars."

"Should I sell them?"

"What have you in mind?"

"I'll be opening a millinery, but I need help to see that I don't get cheated for rent."

"You should sell some of this stock, but I would definitely keep some as well. If you like I'll investigate suitable shop rentals, but it'll cost you a fee commensurate with my time."

There was a knock on the outer office door.

"Excuse me." He opened the door, admitting a handsome young man with blond curly hair, dressed in the shirt and pants of a miner.

"I'm sorry to interrupt," he said, glancing appreciatively at Resa, "but I wanted to stop by. Is there anything I can do for you while you're down below?"

"Claude, this is Mrs. Cluvier. A widow. She's about to hire me to help her find a reasonable rental for her business."

Claude shook Resa's hand. "A pleasure, ma'am."

"As you heard, I leave for San Francisco on this afternoon's stage," Augustus Colbert turned to Resa.

"But I need an opinion on the store soon," she said.

"Claude, would you be willing to help Mrs. Cluvier?" To Resa he said, "My son's an engineer at the Yellow Jacket. I'm sure he can do a good job."

I'll bet he can. Resa smiled at Claude.

"I work the day shift. If you like, I can meet you at your hotel around three-thirty tomorrow, unless you're still in mourning."

"I'm staying at the Sharon House," Resa replied. "When I came here I put away my weeds."

"I'll meet you in the lobby at three-thirty, then."

Augustus escorted her to the door.

"Thank you," she said warmly.

"Don't mention it . . . oh, Claude, stay for a moment. I'll need some help while I'm gone."

'I'm no longer in mourning.' If you only knew what I've worn black for. She hummed as she strolled along. *I hope you're single, Claude Colbert.*

Chapter Fifteen

At half past three the following day, Resa and Claude met in the Sharon House lobby. Maria sat in a leather chair watching them. Too late, Resa noticed that the newspaper she held in front of her face was upside down. Maria dropped it to her lap and stared at Claude suspiciously. Then she nodded to Resa. She relaxed her arm, which had momentarily gone for the derringer in her skirt pocket.

"We'll go straight to see Baxter Thistle. He's a notorious smooth dealer. I arranged for him to meet us at the shop." Claude took Resa's arm, guiding her over the rough boardwalk, past a legless miner, his stumps setting on a cart, who propelled himself along with his arms. Each hand held a leather-covered plunger. In front of him, strapped to the cart, a box of fresh apples proclaimed his livelihood. "Apples," he called. "Fresh from Carson Valley . . . ripe, juicy apples."

Resa was transfixed by the man's retreating back. Claude gently guided her onward.

"Armless and legless men are common enough," he said. "Cables snap. Rocks fall."

"He's no older than I." She shivered.

"Any miner's older than God."

In front of the shop next to the Last Chance, a pudgy, red-faced man with thick glasses and a derby lounged against the wall. He wore a green and purple plaid coat and chomped a cigar. From his pocket a heavy gold watch fob dangled. He drew out a large watch and glanced nervously at the time.

"Mr. Thistle?" Claude reached out his

hand. "This is Mrs. Stafford Cluvier, the lady whom I mentioned."

"Yessirree. Always a pleasure." He tipped his hat to Resa and bowed at the waist. "Yessiree."

Resa had the feeling he had measured her hips precisely when he bowed. Instantly, she loathed him, his squinty eyes and his loud clothing.

Thistle produced a set of keys and unlocked the door. Inside, the walls were covered with faded paper in an erratic rose and violet pattern. From the high ceiling a utility lamp hung forlornly. The shop smelled of shoe polish and of cat droppings.

"Yessiree, it's one of my best. Was a shoe shop 'til the owner passed on." He rubbed his hands unctuously.

"How much per month?" asked Resa. They were standing behind a high shelf, made for shoe boxes, that separated the front of the shop from the back. In the back room was a small oak desk, a high table for ledgers, a high stool, and a stove.

"Twenty-five," said Thistle.

"Twenty-five is too dear," said Claude.

"Will you accept twenty dollars?" negotiated Thistle. "It won't last long. Already a jeweler's made me an offer."

Resa glanced at Claude. He nodded imperceptibly.

"Yes. Twenty will be fine if you will supply me three or four more lamps for the counters. And promise to have it repapered within six months."

"Done," said Thistle, holding out his hand.

"Please put the terms in writing," said Claude.

"Oh, certainly. Rent's due the first of each month. I'll have the papers for you. Here's the key." He unhooked it and gave it to Resa. "Yessiree, if there's anything you need, you let me know." He bowed again and walked away.

"What a loathsome man," Resa said, relieved that Thistle was finally gone.

"Yessiree," Claude smiled. "Let's eat at the Sharon."

After a dinner of sole, Claude motioned to the waiter and ordered brandy and a cigar with coffee.

"Lots of money and few diversions make fat bellies." Claude pushed his chair back, stretching his legs. He lit his cigar.

The way he wore his clothes—a brown leather jacket and beautifully tailored wool trousers of gun-metal gray—made Resa too aware of his athletic body.

He blew a smoke ring toward the chandelier above the table. The cigar's aroma was elegant, compelling. They watched the ring ascend, distort like a bent flapjack, and dissipate in the brass curlicues of the lamp.

"You should keep your stocks in the California. There's great promise in that mine."

"Maybe," Resa said vaguely.

"I'm surprised you want to enter the world of business," Claude commented.

"Fortunes change. I'll not trust to luck."

He stared intently into her eyes. Resa, uncomfortable, babbled.

"For certain it's an adventure. In San Francisco, my friend Maria and I went into the Barbary Coast to a hat manufacturer. It was awful."

Claude sipped his brandy.

"There was a diseased blind man sitting in a doorway, shaking a tin cup, begging. Maria drew out her knife as we walked past a row of red light houses."

Claude smiled.

"Even though it was morning there was a tune coming from one of them. Jangling out of the fog."

A couple with three children entered the room. The youngest, a girl in white organdy, held a shiny black rock.

"Here, pretty lady." The girl gave the rock to Resa.

"Molly, don't bother the lady." The child's mother looked apologetically at Resa, as she took the girl's hand and led her toward a table.

"Thanks." Resa blushed, and set the rock on the table.

"Child's got taste." Claude held up his glass.

"Back to San Francisco. We passed a Chinese vegetable vendor, a Chinese laundry. Everything began to smell of garlic and ginger. In the shops there was dried squid, fresh chicken blood and gray-green pork bladders. Out front, haggling over a cart of half-rotted fish, were a group of disreputable looking women."

"What a place," Claude said, enchanted with the music of Resa's voice.

"Yet worst of it all was the shop. We found it in a terrible alley hung with laundry. Sitting on a walkway above us a Chinese woman dangled her legs and nodded. She must have been drugged. She was nursing a baby. I swear she was an inch from oblivion.

"Inside, a Chinese who spoke English, took us to the display room. It was off the sweatshop. We had to walk through it. You never saw such a den. Poor women bent over sewing machines in semi-darkness. They were surrounded by fabric, thread, spools, and cards of needles.

"And the stench. It reeked of sizing and of sweat.

"At the front of the room a giant urged the women on. I'm certain they were beaten if they lost a moment's time. They looked like animals burrowing among the hat forms, sewing on feathers, geegaws, sequins. Everything was helter-skelter on the tables.

"Right then and there I decided San Francisco wasn't for me. Yet, frightful as it was, I'm glad I got my hats. When I went back with the muleskinner to get my order, I took my Sharps. And I counted everything right in the wagon."

Claude puffed on his cigar, and said, "The mines are no picnic either. I was at the five-hundred foot level one afternoon when a man fell from two hundred. We heard him screaming, then nothing. By the time he stopped, his arms, legs, head were gone . . . truth is, I hate the mines."

"You could leave," Resa suggested gently.

"My father spent a fortune educating me. He's sure I'll find the next bonanza. I don't stay because of him, though. The earth's a challenge. There are ways to make it safer for the men who have no choice, if the owners can be convinced to pay attention."

"Sounds like a useless crusade."

"Sometimes when I'm down there, I'd give anything to have a ranch. Space. Fresh air. I dream of cattle, maybe some grapes."

Resa reached across the table and squeezed his hand in hers.

"To your business," Claude said and raised his glass. "I wish my fiancée had your sand. But she's delicate, born with a silver spoon."

Resa's heart leapt to her throat. She surprised herself when she said in a normal voice, "Then there's no need for strength, I suppose."

"Still," Claude said, "I'd feel better if she weren't so frail. Her name's Fanny Frazier. I think you'd like her." He pushed back his chair.

As they left, Resa said, "Come by the shop tomorrow, I'll have your commission then." She still held the shiny black rock.

The following morning, Resa, with the help of the hotel clerk, hired two men to move the goods from the Sharon to the shop. All morning they hauled boxes and furniture to the store. They put the goods in the back room and placed the heavy display cases near the walls. Resa and Maria donned aprons and scrubbed the shop until the fixtures shone. Then they swept and mopped the floors, and cleaned the display cases until they gleamed. By early afternoon, the movers were finished. The goods awaited arranging. Most of the cat smell was drowned under a haze of ammonia, but the shoe polish odor remained.

The October wind howled.

"Winter's coming," said Maria as they rested before unpacking the boxes. "It'll be hard for business."

"I thought of that. We'll get some delicate cakes and cookies from next door, and keep a pot of tea water on the stove. I'll buy a cunning cup rack and cups so the ladies can have refreshments while they shop. A sofa. I'll need a sofa and some comfortable chairs."

"Iron's hot," said Maria, spitting on the plate that rested on the small stove in the back room.

"I'll unpack. We'll press one box at a time."

"Hate it. Why do Anglos need flimsy wrinkly things, anyway? My people always managed to do it without yards of lace."

"All this delicate folderol makes the ladies feel delicate. Just like Claude Colbert's delicate fiancée. Who am I to argue with fashion?" said Resa, trying to sound lighthearted.

They took turns pressing flannel nightgowns, lawn nightgowns; robes, in chalice, velvet, and crepe with rows of lace; and filmy camisoles with mother-of-pearl buttons. They unpacked gloves, parasols and pearl-handled button hooks. Every item was a delight to Resa. They made her dream of France. They smelled of money and of clipper ships.

By late afternoon, they had a representative selection of stock out. Resa opened one particularly fine selection of hats. These she put on the hall tree at the shop's entrance where they could be seen from the street.

"That's enough for today," she said to Maria. "Bank the fire and we'll go."

Just then she heard a terrible snarling. She turned. Outside Claude pointed at a huge black beast of a dog. "Stay! You renegade son of a mongrel! Stay!"

Resa opened the door.

"We were just getting ready to close. I'm glad you came."

"Mrs. Cluvier, I want you to meet Sir

Galahad." He pointed to the dog, who growled at Resa, baring his teeth. "Sir, this is Mrs. Cluvier."

"Claude, please. Come in. I'll get you your money."

Sir Galahad growled again. As Claude entered, the dog bolted around his legs and went thrashing through the shop, almost upsetting Maria as she came out of the back, her arms laden with gowns. He jumped on Maria, who threw the gowns into the air.

"You! Ruin my work!" She shoved the dog off and stood with her arms raised above him.

"Get out!" Claude rushed to Sir, grabbed him by the scruff of the neck and hauled him back to the street, shutting the door firmly behind him.

Maria brushed herself off and bent to pick up the gowns. "We eat them. Loco! *Ptui!*" she spat.

"I'm sorry. He's nobody's friend but mine, I'm afraid." Claude helped a swearing Maria pick up the gowns. They introduced themselves.

Resa laughed. Claude looked ludicrous with his arms full of lacy things. She took them from him and hung them. Then she went to the back room and returned with her handbag.

Claude was standing admiring a hat on the hall tree. It was one of the most expensive ones—a gray velvet tricorn with ostrich feathers sweeping back to front.

"Fanny'd love this," he said, stroking the feathers.

"Take it," said Resa. "It's yours, provided Miss Frazier tells everybody where she got it."

She handed him his money. "Wait, I have something for your friend, too." She went into the back. At the bottom of a box was a buckram hat frame that hadn't survived the Sierras. It was bent and soiled. Resa brought it out.

"Give it to Sir Galahad. He needs something to sweeten his temper."

"I got a telegram from father, today. He'll be back next Monday." Claude opened the door. Carefully, Resa and Maria followed. He gave the hat to Sir Galahad. He snarled at it for a moment, then began chewing it with relish. The trio watched him as he demolished it—tearing it to pieces, nosing it, flinging bits of buckram into the breeze.

"Hey, Colbert. That's the first time I ever saw that brute content," called a miner from across the street.

"It's amazing," said Claude. "Thanks for the money, by the way."

"I hate to ask more favors, but when the shop is open, Maria and I'll need a house. Will you help me find one?"

"Sure. Will you and Maria join me for dinner?"

"No, thanks. Your fiancée might object. Besides, it's been a long day."

Sir Galahad finished his hat. As Resa and Maria watched him walk away with Claude, nosing at the velvet masterpiece in its hatbox, Resa laughed.

"Ain't I the proper one?" Resa joshed. "Let's go get a soak for our feet."

Men in the doorways doffed their hats as she and Maria passed. By the time they reached the hotel, Resa was full of bubbling satisfaction.

Chapter Sixteen

Whether he dreamed of more buckram hats or he entertained other dog ideas, Sir Galahad stationed himself daily at the door of Resa's shop. He would arrive about ten in the morning, tousled from a fight or panting from a game of rabbit chase, and spread out, his gigantic blackness filling the doorway. He had Comstock ethics, for he growled and bared his teeth at passing miners, but pretended sleep whenever a lady entered the shop. He howled with the whistles that signalled the change of shifts, raising his blunt nose toward the sky. Sometimes he'd leave for a while at midday, exploring other possibilities, but within a week the shop, which Resa christened The Gilded Cage, became his home away from home. Both Resa and Claude were trained to his habit. Resa began bringing him a tidbit or two from the Sharon House kitchen; Claude habitually stopped by to pick him up after work.

One morning, a couple of weeks later, a messenger boy arrived at the door of the shop. Sir, true to his cantankerous nature, growled and refused to let the boy inside. Resa saw him. She opened the door, took Sir Galahad by the scruff of the neck and held him while the boy delivered his message. It was a request that she meet with Augustus Colbert in his office at three o'clock. She gave an affirmative reply, tipped the lad, and sent him on his way.

"He's such a bad dog," she said to Maria when she went back inside. "Yet I feel safer having him here. Augustus Colbert will think I can't write. It was either give the boy a verbal answer or have him chewed to pieces."

Maria was cutting yards upon yards of tulle into scarf lengths. "When he sees the ladies with their hat-scarves he'll know you're smart."

"It was a good idea. Giving away a scarf to keep hats tied on. Oh, I'm clever." She twirled around the floor, but stopped short when two women came in to buy gloves.

That afternoon, she entered Colbert's office. Again, she waited patiently while he looked through papers for several minutes before he turned his attention to her.

"I had a profitable trip to San Francisco," he said in answer to her inquiry. "I've been here for eight years, but I still can't believe how much money's to be gotten from these hills, from the stocks.

"That's why I've called you here. I've given the matter of your stocks thorough consideration. It would be madness for you to cash them in now. You stand to double or even triple your money with the railroad to Carson coming."

"Nevertheless, Mr. Colbert, I've decided to sell all my stocks except the California. Will you sell them for me?"

"Mrs. Cluvier, when Fr. Bernard sent you to me, I thought it was for you to take my advice. Apparently I was wrong."

"You're not wrong. I like my money to be where I can see it."

He smiled. His body seemed to grow as he puffed before her. She thought of a dragon, spewing its fire over the room, and would have been amused had his eyes not been so cold.

"I feel I'm cheating you to complete such a transaction. I've built this firm on my handshake and intuition. I've made myself and many others very wealthy. You won't reconsider?"

"No. When can I have the cash?"

He paused. "Day after tomorrow. Drop by in the afternoon. I'll have it for you then." He stood. He was still breathing fire. She felt it scorch her back as she left the room.

"Your father was angry with me when I told him to sell my stocks," said Resa to Claude when he came to get Sir Galahad.

"He hates to lose. Especially when he thinks he can make a client money. He huffs and blusters, but he's a fine person, really. It's just that he's so enthusiastic about the Comstock.

"When he moved from Boston to California in '50, he was one of a crowd of lawyers. Now, between his dealings in California and here, he has power, prestige

216

and money. I guess I can't blame him for his enthusiasm."

"You came from Boston?"

"Yes. When I was five. I scarcely remember anything about the trip around the horn. But my mother was sick the whole time."

"The trip west made me sick, too."

"I've been talking with Fr. Bernard. His sister, Madelaine Doyle, is having a party on Sunday. He asked if I'd invite you. You can't miss the house. It's that brick mansion on B Street with columns on the porch. Fanny will be there."

"Maria and I'd love to come. I look forward to meeting Fanny."

"It's at five in the evening."

"See you there." She stared after them as Claude and Sir Galahad wandered up the street.

"I'd rather be facing a bar full of drunks," Resa whispered to Maria as they walked up the steps to the Doyle mansion that Sunday. The house was as big as their hotel. It glistened, white, against the barren brown of the hills.

"Do I look all right? How's my hat? My hair?" She wiggled beneath her navy faille cape with silk roses at the throat.

"Fine. After three hours of primping, you should. Don't get so het up. You can do anything." Maria brushed an imaginary speck from Resa's shoulder as they rang the bell.

They were greeted at the door by the butler. He took the invitation Fr. Bernard had given her that morning, put it on a silver calling-card tray shaped like a peacock that set on a marble stand. A maid took their wraps, revealing Maria's dark blue crepe and Resa's high-throated pink silk with lace at the collar and cuffs. As the butler turned to lead them into the parlor, Resa grasped Maria's hand. She was almost overwhelmed by the wallpaper on which fleur de lis boats sailed a green ocean of waterwave silk. A brass hall-tree on which were dried flowers jutted into the room, next to which sat a teak umbrella stand, and a marble-topped table.

In the parlor, the butler announced them.

"There you are," said Fr. Bernard, who set down his thimble of sherry. "Come, Mrs. Cluvier, I want you to meet my sister, Madelaine."

He guided her and Maria through the throng.

"Who's this beauty?" called a young man

to Fr. Bernard.

"In a moment, Jasper. We'll be right back."

Resa was conscious of eyes scanning her from head to foot. Her palms were cold. She fought a desire to wrap her arms around herself. Maria responded to the stares by looking right back, seeing if Resa needed defending. She was glad the knife rested against her leg, even though Resa had talked her out of wearing her derringer.

"They're just another bunch of Anglos," she had said to Resa before they left the Sharon. "Money doesn't make them tame; it just hides them better."

"Thank God it hasn't made you tame, but if you draw that sticker short of a war, I'll send you back to Santa Fe."

"Maybe after you find new rich friends you'll wish you had."

"Nonsense." Resa had hugged her.

They entered the center of the coterie.

"Madelaine, this is Mrs. Stafford Cluvier, the widow I've told you about. And her companion, Miss Maria Sanchez. Resa, this is my sister Madelaine and her husband,

Thadeus Doyle."

Both Madelaine and Doyle extended their hands. He wore thick glasses that made him look drowsy. He was unprepossessing for a mining baron.

"May I get you something? Coffee? Sherry?" asked Madelaine politely. Resa surveyed the room. She saw sherry glasses in the ladies' hands.

"A sherry, thank you," she said cordially. Doyle poured her a thimble, leaving Madelaine free to pour tea or coffee from huge silver services on either end of the oval coffee table. A maid stood by waiting to replenish refreshments. Madelaine was a large woman, though not heavy. Like Fr. Bernard, she had red hair. Her long nose hardened her appearance so that the scalloped trim on her maroon gown looked like a fence enclosing a porcupine.

"I hope you and Maria will enjoy the music. Our children will sing, and we've arranged for a Beethoven sonata. We've only recently enlarged our solarium."

"I haven't heard Beethoven since I left New Orleans," said Resa delightedly. "Such a treat."

"Mrs. Cluvier." Resa turned. Claude Colbert came toward her. A mouse of a girl in white hung on his arm.

He introduced her as Fanny Frazier. *'Delicate' isn't half of it. She's wizened.* Resa extended her hand to Fanny. Her touch was firm as a man's, to Resa's surprise.

"Claude, let me serve you. Then will you please show Mrs. Cluvier and Miss Sanchez the solarium?" Madelaine said.

"Claude tells me of your business," Fanny said in a thin voice. "How adventurous of you."

"Our bonnets and gloves are from my stock. If you like them, I'd be happy to have your trade."

"They're lovely. However, I have plenty. But thank you for the gray hat."

Fanny gestured with her left hand. A large diamond on her ring finger caught the light and glistened. Resa hated the ring and immediately thought it gaudy.

"To the solarium." Claude handed Fanny her demitasse.

As splendid as the parlor and entry hall were, the solarium was even more elegant. It was a dream world. On the south side of the mansion, its walls were made of panes of glass. It sparkled against the dark colors of the rest of the decor like a jewel set in black marble. Banked around the room were potted orange trees. Flowers—impatience, geraniums, others Resa didn't know—

bloomed in pots. Outside it was blustery. Inside, the blues and reds and yellows of the flowers made the room as warm as an adobe in late spring. Rows of padded green and white chairs circled the room. In the center of the circle stood a grand piano.

Twenty or thirty guests sipped their drinks, awaiting the performance. The melody of conversation bounced off leaves and played among the flowers, like violins in a jungle.

"Fancy," Resa commented to Fanny.

"San Francisco houses are grander," Fanny said.

At that moment six children filed in, ranging from age eight to perhaps eighteen. Thadeus Doyle introduced them as his own. *No wonder Madelaine is so serious.* Resa set her glass down on a cunning shelf provided on the back of the chair in front of her. *Scarcely a year between them.*

The oldest girl, about Resa's age, with her mother's long nose and her red hair done up—signaling her eligibility—played the piano. The second, a boy, played a violin. The children, rehearsed to their eyebrows, mechanically forced their way through "Open Thy Lattice, Love," "De Camptown Races," "Nelly Bly," and "Massa's in the Cold, Cold Ground," finishing with "Home

Sweet Home." Then, precisely bowing to whistles and applause, they filed out of the room.

"I miss children," said Maria. "Could I play with them?"

Resa walked to Fr. Bernard's chair. "Would Mrs. Doyle be upset if Maria visits the children?" she asked.

"No. I'll take her to them. Though she'll find they're hellions, I fear." He smiled.

Maria left with Fr. Bernard, her bulk struggling behind him. Resa went back to her seat just as a woman dressed in a heavy green velvet gown entered and seated herself at the piano. She was followed by a tiny man with a violin. People had been staring at Maria as she left. Resa didn't like it.

"Your friend's not ill, I hope," whispered Fanny as Thadeus Doyle droned through the introductions.

"No. She wants to visit the children."

"That's no doubt more to her liking," Fanny smiled.

Throughout the sonata Resa thought about Maria. Maria had tried to beg out of the party, but Resa had talked her into it. *We've been through thick and thin. Let's share the good times, too.* Yet she felt uncomfortable, and knew Maria's discomfort must be worse.

Across the room sat Augustus Colbert and a rail-thin woman with pince-nez attached to a heavy gold chain. She was dressed in black, a shriveled shrew. Augustus caught Resa's eye, and returned a smile, a mingling of suspicion and lechery. Resa turned her head. *How such a handsome man as Claude ever happened to them. Old goat. He's dangerous, a fatter T. J. Pryne.*

An old woman in lavender silk nodded sleepily in front of her. Resa could hear men's shoes scraping quietly, yet impatiently aginst the tiles. *They're as bored if not as uncomfortable as I.*

After the music, supper was served. Yet Maria didn't join her. Fr. Bernard sat to her right; a young man, Jasper Fantana, sat to her left. He wore a dapper gray suit. On his cuffs were heavy gold cuff links set with garnets. He had the blackest eyes Resa had ever seen. They shone like the garnets in his cuff links as he talked with her.

After the fish course, Fantana stood and raised his glass. "I propose a toast to Resa Cluvier, the lovely new lady in our midst. She'll be the countess of the Comstock in no time at all."

The company toasted Resa while her cheeks blazed.

"Watch that Fantana," a man down the

table called to Resa. "He's Rumanian. They're the most romantic men in the world, I'm told."

Everyone laughed.

"He'll woo you, it's certain," said a bald-headed fellow. "If you hear a violin caterwauling outside your window, you'll know he's scraping his love song for you."

"It's gypsy music, not caterwauling," Jasper smiled good-naturedly.

"It's heard all over the city, whenever he's in love, which is about three times a month," said the bald man.

"A gypsy lover. I'll bet you have girls lined up for miles around," Resa jested.

"What girls? They're rare as hen's teeth in this pit of a place. The boys know how lonely I am, how lonely we all are. They're jealous I'm seated by you." He bantered on. Everyone obviously liked him. Resa did as well.

"Do you ride, Resa?" he asked.

"Not since I left New Orleans, I'm afraid. I love it, though."

"We must ride then."

"I'd like that. But I work six days a week so Sunday is my only free day."

"You work?" he asked, surprised.

She explained. They arranged to ride the following Sunday afternoon.

"That battle-worn Chileano or Indian or whatever she is . . ." Fanny's voice broke like glass shattering in Resa's ear. Fanny was laughing with Augustus who sat across from her.

"Are you talking about Maria?"

"Charity, Fanny," chided Fr. Bernard.

"Yes, I was talking about Miss Sanchez." Fanny flushed red. "There's no culture when an Indian can visit in the best houses."

Resa stood. Everyone in the room turned toward her.

"Maria may be battle-worn, but she is my friend and companion. I will not stand to hear her insulted."

She pushed back her chair. The guests were dead silent as she walked to the head of the table. Her shaking knees threatened the upward tilt of her chin.

"Mr. Doyle, Mrs. Doyle I've enjoyed your party. But I must go. Miss Frazier has a guttersnipe's manners. Will you please ask someone to find my friend Maria?"

Stunned, Madelaine Doyle motioned to a maid. As she walked from the dining room, Resa held her head high.

She heard the rush of conversation as she waited for Maria in the entryway. The butler stood by the front door as though made of marble.

Maria came down the stairs, looking left and right for trouble, ready to draw her knife. The butler helped them on with their cloaks. Soon they were walking toward the Sharon. It had started snowing.

"If they can applaud the screeching of the Doyle kids and be nasty about you, to hell with the lot of them," Resa seethed.

But Maria said nothing.

The next day two large bouquets arrived at Resa's room. One, of daisies and stock, bore a card that said, "Courage. I'll see you Sunday." It was signed by Jasper Fantana. The second, a selection of yellow roses, bore the message, "Bravo, Resa!" It came from Claude Colbert.

"It's war with Fanny Frazier," Resa laughed as she showed Maria the cards. She danced around the room aping Fanny and Augustus. She put a rose between her teeth and did a wild tarantella.

"War. Do you hear me? War!"

Maria patted her side where she always wore her knife, and smiled.

Chapter Seventeen

The snow that began after Resa and Maria left Doyles continued for two days. The world was blanketed with white that covered the log piles, making frosted mountains of them, that blotted out the dumps, that frosted everything ugly under a beautiful, strangling cover.

"It's a good thing I got in plenty of

wood," Resa said to Maria. "The stoves, the tea and cakes will make all the difference in business."

But business didn't come.

For four days, she and Maria plowed to The Gilded Cage and sat idly all day. The only businesses that were thriving were the saloons. Music from the Last Chance reminded them that some lines of work profited from the snow. Millinery wasn't one of them.

"Bet the houses are hopping." Maria lifted her eyes from her sewing.

"It better break soon or by spring we'll be eating our stock." Resa was lettering a sign, "Warm gloves, flannels," to put in the window.

"I'll advertise in the *Enterprise*, too." She held up the sign, studying its lettering.

By the fourth day, business improved a little. Some ladies, whom Resa recognized from the Doyles', came in to buy mufflers and the fur-lined gloves that Resa had touted in the paper. The sun shone brightly, but it was so cold that the air crackled.

The women tried on hats, not serious about buying. "Got to do something to pass the time," said one, as she slapped a bright red bonnet over her white curls.

"Genevieve, you look like a Fair but Frail

in that contraption," said her companion. Resa cast a meaningful glance at Maria.

The shop door opened. Four women walked past Sir Galahad, giggling. As their eyes grew used to the darkness, their giggles ceased as though chopped off with a knife. They stood politely on the side of the room opposite the ladies.

"Come, Genevieve. The air in here reeks." The older woman barely gave Genevieve time to take off the hat. She practically dragged her out of the shop past the women. Sir Galahad growled at their departing forms.

"May I help you?" asked Resa.

"Sure, honey. We're just itching to spend some of this loot. It's been a hell of a week." The tallest woman, dressed in lavender, began looking at the gowns in the cases.

"Yeah. Busiest week since Fourth of July," said a plump blond.

Resa opened the case and brought out several gowns.

"Oh, look at this bonnet, will you?" An ugly stringy black-haired shrew gabbled. "I've got to have it. Lordy it was nice of you to let us come, Madam Sophie."

"You need the air," said Sophie, who lounged against the hall tree, not interested in buying.

"I wish Cindy had come with us. She's

feeling poorly. If you ask me, she's mad at Big Eddie Greebe for raising her cut."

"He and that damned Colbert. It's worse all the time. They don't leave us nothing," said the tall girl.

"What's this Cindy look like?" asked Maria.

"We call her Red. She's tall. Rawboned-like. Reddest head of hair never came out of a bottle."

"Shut up," said Sophie to her girls.

Colbert. Cindy with bright red hair. Resa grabbed the edge of the case.

"I want this gown," said the blond. She held it up against her and handed it to Resa. "And that robe."

"No. I want the robe. It's better with my coloring," the girl in lavender said.

"You always get blue and this time I want it."

"I have one just like this in a paler shade," said Resa.

"Let Pauline have the dark one," said Sophie. "You take the lighter, Mag."

"You always give her what she wants. Why can't I have it?" She pushed Pauline out of the way and grabbed the dark blue gown from Resa's hands, ripping the sleeve.

Pauline attacked her, struggling for the robe.

"Ladies! Ladies!" Sophie shouted. "One

more move out of either of you, you go back without anything."

"No! You tear up the merchandise, you buy it!" Resa was shaking with fury.

"We'll settle this later," said Madam Sophie. She looked at Resa apologetically as Resa began wrapping the packages.

Like treed cats, Pauline and Mag faced each other. Only Sophie's threatening glance kept them from having a free-for-all.

In the chilled silence a siren could be heard and bells clanged.

"My God," said Sophie. "It must be a good one." She thrust money from her purse into Resa's hand.

"Let's go. Sounds like it's coming from the C & C."

The women rushed out into the street. Men poured out of the Last Chance, out of the bakery, out of businesses along the way. Everyone rushed down the steep hill, as fast as the icy streets would let them, past St. Mary's, where they could see three white ambulance wagons rushing along the bench below the C & C toward the hospital. On the streets below them, people ran out of their houses. It seemed the whole population of Virginia City was sliding toward the C & C. Fire engines, pulled by horses, slid from the south toward the mine. Another engine, bell clanging, pushed through the crowds from C Street, its driver swearing at people who wouldn't move.

Resa and Maria pushed forward.

People pushed toward the C & C entrance. Out of the door came two men, carrying a third on a stretcher. They walked through a miners' cordon—men ringed tightly at the entrance to the hoist house.

"It's Joe McKinnan," somebody called. A woman rushed toward the stretcher. Two children followed her. When she saw her man, she cried out. The ambulance driver held her back while they loaded her husband. Then he mounted the ambulance and drove off. The woman and children followed it, running down the canyon. The stretcher bearers went back into the hoist house, ignoring the pleas of women who thrust out their arms, begging for news. It was a cacophony of calling women, of anxious men, yet none of the men surrounding the door said anything.

For a long while, it seemed, the door stayed closed.

At the 800 level Claude staggered up from the floor. He had been knocked half-senseless by a piece of falling rock. His shoulder was bruised and scraped. His chest and arm were scalded. All along the drift he could hear cries and screams. In the semi-darkness, he ran toward the cage, fleeing to outdistance the boiling water, the steam that spewed out from the face, maybe sixty feet from where he had been standing and supervising a crew repairing square sets when the explosion roared through the drift.

Penrose followed him, going the other way.

"It's Fenno's crew. They're stuck in there. Donegal's too."

Claude wheeled and followed Penrose back toward the face.

The farther in they went, the hotter it got. They could hear steam hissing and water gushing ahead. The odor of sulphur was overpowering.

"Help me! Son of a bitch! Help me!"

Penrose and Colbert squinted their eyes against the heat and groped down the tunnel.

"Fenno?"

"Get me out. The others are gone. Drowned. My legs! Steam! So fast! The gas."

"Get him out of his pants," Penrose yelled.

"No. They've got to be cut off. You one side, me the other."

When they lifted Fenno onto his feet, he screamed, then passed out.

They balanced Fenno between them.

234

Coughing with the fumes, they dragged him toward the cage. As they reached the cage, two hundred feet from the face, a siren wailed eerily in the darkness above them.

The cage was up.

The water was already two inches deep.

"Climb the frame," Claude yelled. Penrose hoisted Fenno over his shoulder and leaped onto the heavy timbers.

Claude coughed. The gas was getting worse. He jerked the bell line. Again, then harder, trying to signal the cage. He struggled and helped Penrose hold Fenno.

They hung there, fear of the water outweighing their fear that the cage would scrape them off the frame and send them plummeting below.

The cables moved at last. The cage descended.

They dumped Fenno onto the floor, then jumped in themselves. Claude jerked the bell line as the water began seeping into the wood floor. The cage jerked. Claude and Penrose sank to the floor, next to Fenno. He moaned. Penrose and Claude were silent.

"Let's go back," said Resa.

"You go on. I'm going to stretch my legs." Maria walked down the hill.

Resa turned and was starting away when

the C & C door opened again. Colbert walked out, shirtless and filthy. His hat was slammed on his head like a pancake.

Through the cordon he walked, stunned.

"There's one of the goddamned engineers," a miner yelled.

"You're supposed to prevent messes like this," a woman screamed. She started toward Colbert, as if to attack him.

Resa pushed through to him. He was surrounded by the mob. His right arm hung limply at his side. It was red, blistered. He stood there and said nothing.

Resa took his hand.

"Can't you see he's hurt?" she turned, and yelled at the crowd. "Get away! Get away!" She kicked her way through the people and led Claude up the hill, back to the shop. Some of the mob followed, yelling obscenities. As they neared the shop, Sir Galahad charged the crowd. A black ball of fury, he took on the mob. Only then did they back off and scatter down the hill.

Resa led Claude inside, hastily locked the door and took him to the back room. She pointed him to the chair by the fire.

"Oh, God. My God, it was awful!" His head was between his hands. He stared at ghosts.

"You need a drink. Some doctoring. Sit

still. I'll be right back."

She ran to the pharmacist's on C Street. She grabbed a roll of gauze off a shelf. "I'm Resa Cluvier. I'll pay for this later," she yelled to the startled pharmacist.

She ran back down the hill to the Last Chance. Resa paid no attention to the startled faces of the men when she poured two drinks from the bottle at the bar. "I'll bring the glasses back and pay for this in a few minutes," she called as she tucked the gauze under one arm and balanced the drinks in her hands.

Back in the shop, she handed the whiskey to Claude. He drained them both. Then he put his head back in his hands.

"God in Heaven," he shook his head back and forth.

"How many dead?"

"I'm not sure. Twenty at least, not counting those that'll die later. The face was a cauldron."

His shoulders heaved. He cried. "Fenno's my best friend. Hell of an engineer."

"Thank God you're alive," Resa said.

"It was Fenno got Quin to borrow me from the Jacket to work on that rotted porphyry."

Resa cut the gauze, wound it around his shoulder, down his arm, and to his fingers.

He winced.

She cradled him in her arms. Rocking him against her waist, absorbing his tears with her skirt. At last he was still. Claude stood up and drew Resa to him with his good arm. He kissed her hard, as though her lips could erase the terror. Resa responded as she hadn't since the days she'd loved Boone.

Outside, Sir Galahad barked.

"Hell of it is, all I could think of was getting out," he said, as he held Resa tightly, smelling the fragrant scent of her hair. "Oh, if my father and the others would only listen to Sutro, half the casualties might never have happened. A tunnel would have meant safety, venting, an escape for the water, steam, gas.

"Damn them. Who cares about those miners? About their children, their widows? Who in hell has the time to care? Damn all of us in our greed." He kissed her again.

Then, as though aware of his surroundings for the first time, he stopped, and drew back from her.

"I . . ." She covered his lips with her fingers.

"Shhh. Whatever you say'll not be right. Go now. When this nightmare's past, we'll talk."

Chapter Eighteen

Virginia City was in mourning. The obituaries in the *Territorial Enterprise* read like an international congress of grief. Fate had been impartial, drawing to its bosom miners of Irish, Cornish, Welsh, German, French, Italian, and Swedish ancestry— thirty-two in all. Funeral bells clanged from every church in the city. Nature, as though wishing to compound the grief, let loose with two days of a blizzard that made burials impossible. Even in the saloons, no amount of liquor could erase the sorrow, the outrage that the men felt.

Resa felt chilled as she sold the black trappings of death—veils, gloves, black stockings.

When the burials started—five long days after the accident—the processions, wending their way past the skeleton-bare trees of the cemetery, continued for four days. Volunteer crews dug the graves side by side. They were terrible in their gaping grayness. The scars in the snow were pathetic sacrifices to the jealous god of silver.

Jasper Fantana called Resa to the lobby of the Sharon House. He looked haggard, stunned. His black eyes had circles beneath them.

"I lost ten friends," he said. "Ten," he repeated, and paused. "Naturally, I cannot see you this Sunday. The Knights of Columbus are gathering charity packages for the widows."

"I've nothing in my shop that will help much," Resa said, "but I'll give you money. Someone who knows the families can buy what they'll be needing. Wait here."

Outside the storm was raging.

She returned with two hundred-fifty dollars, and handed the sum to Jasper. "It's all the money I have here. Come back after the funerals and I'll give you more when I can get to Wells Fargo."

"The Lord'll bless you for this," Jasper said gratefully.

"The miners' families aren't the only ones bad off," Maria said as her knitting needles clicked amid red yarn. "The people down the canyon need everything. I thought I'd make sweaters for the children."

"When this is over, I've got to get a house, Jasper," Resa said. "We can help more if we're not cooped up in a hotel."

Maria's knitting needles clicked on.

After the funerals the snow continued. Natives said there'd never been a winter like it. Icicles formed solid sheets down the buildings, and soon the whole city looked like a fantasy in ice.

Christmas was muffled, saddened. Resa and Maria went to Mass alone. They spent Christmas day carrying clothes and supplies to the Indians in their shacks. Resa gave Maria a fine blanket from Mexico; Maria gave her a green jacket-sweater that she made herself whenever Resa was out.

Yet tragedy nor weather could extinguish the spirit of the Comstock for long. People simply piled on more wood and allowed themselves extra time for their errands. Hearty souls waded through the snow-choked streets, congratulating themselves that wheeled traffic was at a standstill, and they doubled their loads of provisions to help shut-ins.

Three weeks after the accident, Fantana came into the store on a Saturday. The weather had broken the previous day. The sun shone brightly from a startlingly blue sky.

Sir Galahad, who had vanished for several days, was back at his post. He growled at Fantana, but Resa tossed him an old glove. He was mollified.

"I've found a sled. Will you ride with me tomorrow?" Jasper asked eagerly.

"Hallalujah!" Resa exclaimed. "Anything to get some fresh air."

The following afternoon, bundled under robes, muffled with layers of warm clothing, Fantana and Resa drove north of the city. The sun shone as though trying to make up for lost time. The air was bitter, but, for once, the Washoe zephyr was silenced. The horses pulled the sled—a ponderous affair with wide runners—as

242

though it were a feather. They passed wagons, pulling laboriously up to the high bench before the descent down Geiger Grade. It was exhilarating.

"It's good to be out and away from people," Resa said, her breath clouding the crisp air. "Away from the likes of Fanny Frazier."

"When you picked somebody to tangle with, you started right at the top." Fantana grinned.

"Well, people at the party must agree with me about her," she remarked shrewdly. "The tiff didn't hurt my business."

"The Frazier women are known for making enemies. Fanny's mother moved to San Francisco years ago. She keeps a palace there. Before she got engaged, Fanny would come here to see her father. She always has acted like this is the end of forever. Nobody thought she'd marry. Her tongue's too tart."

"Yet she looks so weak."

"And never have looks so deceived," Jasper said drily.

A rabbit ran out in front of them. They stared after it. Farther on, they came to a large flat place surrounded by small hills. A group of children were sleigh-riding there. They had built a fire near a small abandoned shack with a steep-pitched roof. One boy was turning potatoes under the coals with a long stick.

"It reminds me of upstate New York," said Jasper.

"Do you miss it?"

"No. Back home I'd have died of boredom. Here everything's booming. It changes constantly. There's so much money. Not that New York doesn't have its share, but it's different. There, only a few have it. The little man can't get any."

"So you came west."

"Three years ago. I put all of my money in lumber. First for mine timbering, now I'm waiting for the railroad to Carson. I'm supplying wood. Soon I'll be rolling in clover."

"Here's to our fortunes. I'll take hats, you lay ties. We'll both get rich."

"Here's to the future." Jasper clucked to the horses. They rushed on. "To never going back."

Ahead of them, they saw another party heading in their direction. They slowed to let them pass. In the sled were Claude and Fanny; a black-fringed parasol jogged above her fur hat. A plump young girl and an equally chubby young man sat in back.

As the sled passed theirs, Claude tipped

his hat to Resa. Fanny looked at Resa as though she were a centipede. She was obviously annoyed at Claude. The chubby girl giggled.

"Hey, Colbert," Jasper called. "You want to race?"

"Sure. Around the bowl," Claude called back.

Jasper turned his sled. Side by side the sleds pulled back into the bowl. As they entered the depression, Jasper and Claude yelled to the children to clear the way.

"Three times around. Winner gets twenty," Fantana called. "Hey, boy. Come start us," he called to the potato cooker.

The lad walked to the side of Colbert's sled. He took off his red hat. "When I wave it," he shouted.

"Ready . . . set . . . go!"

They were off! Cheered on by the children, round they went. Fantana's chestnuts pulled ahead only to be passed by Colbert's grays. As they went flying by, Resa noticed that Fanny had her gloves over her eyes. The fat couple was squealing with excitement.

Resa squealed, too, as the sleds almost tangled on the far corner, Fantana and Colbert whipping the straining horses.

Three times around they went. The air rang with their squealing and laughing.

They slid on the ice under the snow. At the end of the race they were in a dead heat.

"Everybody but me and Fantana out," Colbert ordered. "My grays'll take yours with a lighter load."

This time the young man from Colbert's party started them off. As Resa yelled for Fantana, she felt the daggers of Fanny's silence. The light on the snow was blindingly bright. Resa and Fanny stood by the shed, near the fire.

Colbert won. Resa and the others yelled and jumped up and down in the snow. When the men brought their sleds back to the fire, Resa ran forward. As they climbed down to walk the horses, she walked between the men.

"Beautiful!" She gave each man a squeeze. "Can we do this again soon? I love it."

When the horses were cooled down Resa and the men joined the others by the fire. Fantana paid the winnings to Colbert.

"I'll take you on next Sunday. I can't let you get by with this," he smiled.

"Next Sunday it is," said Colbert.

"Darling, don't forget the Clements' opera party for us." Fanny held onto Colbert's arm.

"In two weeks then. Now let's see if these kids have enough potatoes for us, too."

They all ate potatoes. They were steaming and fragrant. The party bounced the hot pieces in their gloved hands. Some of the children went back to sledding. Others examined the horses. Everyone except Fanny borrowed a child's sled and went bellywhomping down the banks.

From her place by the shack, Fanny stared maliciously out at the others. Soon she spit a piece of potato onto the snow.

"Ouch! It burned me!" She jumped up and down. Resa came toward her, laughing.

"Burned myself," Fanny mumbled, luring Resa under the eaves. As she jumped, she scraped the overhanging snow with her parasol. She jumped back. A small avalanche plopped from the roof, covering Resa, burying her where she stood.

"Damnit!" Resa spit snow from her mouth. Everyone laughed as she dusted mounds of it off her coat, her hat, her skirt.

"So sorry," Fanny smiled angelically.

"Let's go," Resa said to Fantana. "By the time we get back, I'll be half-frozen." Everyone got in the sleds. The others sang on the way; but Resa's teeth chattered.

"So you tangled with Virginia City's ice princess." Jasper laughed.

"Pig princess is more like it," Resa said, in a mean temper at the mention of the

247

viper's name.

"If she doesn't get all the attention, she can't stand it," Jasper remarked.

"Thanks for a fine day," Resa said when they pulled up in front of the Sharon. "You're a good friend."

"More than that I hope." He bowed to her as he left her at the stairs. The thought of her covered with snow, snow on her face, under her bonnet, fueled his laughter as he rode back to the livery stable.

"Fanny Frazier, I think you'll meet your match," he roared.

Chapter Nineteen

Resa stood in the back of the shop, brushing her skirt. She was pleased with her navy blue skirt, and with her heavily ruffled waist on which she had placed the amythest pin. Maria sat sewing. She had adopted the Indian children down the canyon. Day and night her needle flew.

"I miss Santa Domingo. I miss the plains.

The buffalo grass, adobe, menudo," Maria intoned sadly.

Resa fingered the amythyst pin. The stone caught the sunlight. *Why should I wear this now? Why should I be thinking of Garcia?*

"I'm going to buy a house. Come spring you can get a horse and ride, Maria."

"It can't come soon enough. Don't buy a fancy house where we need all those waiter people."

"Don't worry," Resa reassured her. "We'll get an elegant place, but small."

"What you do I stick with, but in summer, I'm taking the children to the reservation. I think their mother will be dead by then. She coughs so much. Their father drinks every day. They need a home."

Claude came by after his shift. He and Resa went out and walked through the mire of the January thaw. He clanked several sets of keys together. They saw two houses, neither of which was suitable. At last, near sundown, they found the perfect place. It was recently vacated by the Philpots, who had taken their millions to warmer climes. Mrs. Philpot, not wanting to be bothered with the ordeal of freighting everything over the mountains, had left some heavy furniture behind—a sofa, a headboard, an old rocking chair and a bed.

Otherwise it was empty.

After their tour, Resa stood staring out the bay window, across the hills and the town, toward Sugar Loaf peak.

"You're pensive." Claude stood by her.

"It seems final, somehow. Buying a house."

"You can't live in a hotel forever," he smiled.

"With a house I have to be somebody, maybe somebody I'm not," Resa commented.

"The price is right. You don't have to worry about furnishings. Besides, you should be somebody. You are somebody. One of the most spirited, independent, decent people I've ever known." He reached for her hand. "When I think how you took that dunking from Fanny with such good humor."

She withdrew her hand from his.

"So help me, if . . ." Claude's voice trailed off.

"If?"

"We're to be married in March. Her family and mine have had us planned for years. A great union. Law and mining. Yet . . . when I'm with her I feel as bare as a played-out vein."

"Don't go through with it, then," Resa said.

"My father needs her fortune."

"If you're willing to sell yourself for her money, don't complain to me," Resa said shortly.

"Father's counting on her connections, her money. He plans to run for the Senate. If I back out he'll be furious. And he's not a man to tangle with."

The wheels in Resa's mind turned quickly. She said, "You've still got two months. Find him some new backers and get out. He'll be angry for a while, but he'll accept it."

"And . . . if?"

She took his hand. They looked at the setting sun. The room was rose in its light.

"I loved a man once, Claude," Resa said softly. "I loved him so he made my whole world. Now he's gone. I'll never be a soft thing again. Yet I want a home."

He stroked her neck. His fingers toyed with the hair that fell from her chignon.

"If you break your engagement to Fanny, I'd be lying if I said I wouldn't want to see more of you. You've charm. Intelligence."

He kissed her. Then Claude undid the pins from her hair, scattering them on the floor. He drew her toward the sofa. He played with her curls, then ran his fingers along her arms, reaching for the buttons of her waist.

He covered her face with kisses. "A woman. My God, a woman."

She shook with desire that had died in her in Santa Fe.

Resa pushed herself away from him. Then she crawled on the floor in the dying light, searching for her pins.

She took a deep breath, composing herself, then said, "It's so hard. You'll never know how hard it is . . . but I won't be anybody's whore."

She stood, jamming the pins in the hair she wrapped around her fingers.

Claude stood by her, his arm around her waist. "I won't apologize. Ever since you walked into my father's office, I've wanted nothing but you."

"Then cut your strings," she said.

"Soon. With or without my family's consent."

They walked to the Sharon. Halfway there, Sir Galahad joined them, mud-splattered and torn from a fight.

"Spring's coming. He feels it, too," Resa said.

"You sure say what you mean," Claude smiled, proud that Resa was the woman she was, the woman he wanted.

"Guess my mother died before she made me a lady."

*　　*　　*

Resa told Maria all about the house—and all about the conversation with Claude.

"I want him so bad I can taste it," she confided.

"He's fine. It's time you had someone," Maria lit a cigar.

Resa read the day's *Enterprise* to Maria.

"God in Heaven! Listen to this. 'Cindy Small, recently of Santa Fe, a woman from D Street (the Red Light District), was found dead last night from an overdose of laudanum. Friends said she was despondent over love, alcohol, and financial difficulties.'"

"We're lucky." Maria pulled on her cigar.

"I might be in jail instead of buying a house," Resa said. "Still, I'm sorry she killed herself. Sorrier there was no way out for her. For all of them. I'll send flowers. I wish I could have masses said for her, but I'm afraid."

The following day, Augustus Colbert came to The Gilded Cage. He stared Sir down. He picked out a plain flannel gown, with only a row of buttons on the collar. He looked at robes, but decided against one. Maria finished waiting on two women, then she went to the back.

After the door closed upon the other customers, Augustus said, "I've come to ask you to stay away from my son." Resa wrapped his purchase.

"He's immensely attracted to you," the wealthy man said. "A man would be a fool not to be. Still, I don't want anything getting in the way of his marriage."

"He's his own man, Mr. Colbert," Resa looked him straight in the eye.

"I know your type. You can arrange anything."

"Maybe I don't want to arrange it."

"What is it? Money? Position? I've smelled your kind before. You're all alike. I'll pay, if that's what it takes."

"You've no reason to insult me." In spite of herself, her voice raised. "No. I'll not take money. Just leave me alone."

"Listen well, young lady. I can fix your business, your position. I checked into you. There was never a Stafford Cluvier in New Orleans. I'm certain more digging will open a sewer. What did you do? Steal your money? Kill for it?"

Maria came in from the back. Her derringer was drawn.

"Take your package and go. I won't stand for this," Resa said.

Maria escorted Augustus to the door, prodding his fat sides with the derringer.

Resa laughed to see him leave.

"You didn't need the gun," Resa said,

255

once Colbert's bulk was out the door. "I could've handled him."

"Why pussyfoot with that trash?" Maria went back to her ironing.

"If he's gonna play rough, I'll play rougher. Maria, I want you to go see Madam Sophie. Find out everything you can about the man called Big Eddie, about any relationship he has to Mr. Colbert. Take three hundred-fifty dollars, but don't give her more than one hundred unless she opens up with something we can really use. Don't let anybody see you."

After a little while Jasper Fantana came in. "I've been up at the courthouse checking land titles. It's awfully dull work. When I left, I found this for you."

He pulled the cover, revealing a canary in its cage. "Thought you could use a bird for your Gilded Cage."

"Thanks," Resa said in surprise. "He's a beauty." The bird swung on its perch. It twittered.

"But I'll be moving him soon. I found a house yesterday. We plan to move in a couple of weeks. How'd you like to help?"

"Anything for you," Jasper beamed. "I've another hour or two at work. Will you have dinner with me?"

"Not tonight. After we move I want you to have dinner in my home."

"Grand. I'll trade muscles for home cooking anytime."

Business was brisk. There was false spring warmth in the air. Outside, the melting icicles made rivers in the slush of the streets. The ladies didn't seem to mind the mud. They were buying like fury—bonnets with spring flowers. Resa even sold a couple of pairs of white gloves. Jasper's bird trilled over the sounds of ladies. "Dickie, Dickie," clucked one woman in a green bonnet, wattles vibrating with her imitation of the bird's call.

At about three in the afternoon Maria came back. She came up the back stairs and motioned for Resa.

When Resa was able to get away, Maria said, "Big Eddie runs nine houses. He's the pimp to half the girls on crib row. It took me a bottle of whiskey and the whole three-fifty, but I found out that Sophie thinks Colbert owns all the buildings and takes a cut from the houses. Big Eddie's his front man. I wouldn't have found it out then, but Sophie's angry at them both. Lately, the owners have been taking more than usual, more than they have a right to."

Resa hugged Maria. "Now, if I can just find proof! I'm certain I'm going to need it."

Chapter Twenty

In the days that followed, Resa abandoned the shop to Maria. She checked with painters and paperhangers, with the furniture stores and drapers. Claude gave her advice on prices, but refused to take a fee. The back room of The Gilded Cage became a jumble of fabric samples, lists and geegaws.

Later, in the mornings, she and Maria switched jobs, one cleaning at the house, the other running the store. Afternoons, Resa went to the bank. Later she harassed workmen and supervised as they transformed the house to her taste.

The furniture was to be moved on a Saturday. On Friday, after inspecting the paint and paper for a final time, Resa locked the house and walked back to The Gilded Cage.

"I could eat the biggest steak in Christendom," she said to Maria as they were preparing to close. She surveyed the stock.

"Next week I've got to get some orders out. Though, with the thaw, I'll be lucky to get anything for weeks. The mud is terrible."

"I'd settle for a good bowl of menudo, some tortillas." Maria banked the fire.

The front door opened. Resa went to wait on the customer.

It was Fanny Frazier dressed in a fawn velvet cape and peach silk with a peach parasol.

"May I help you?" Resa asked, chilly, but polite.

"Yes. You two-bit hussy." Fanny spoke between clenched teeth. "Stay away from Claude!" She twirled her parasol. Her eyes glared from narrow slits.

"Claude and I have a business arrangement, no more," Resa said calmly.

"You lie. You lie! Back off. I know your game. It's not going to do you any good. We Fraziers trample dung like you under our horses." She poked the tip of the parasol into Resa's astonished face. Resa jumped back.

"Claude's his own man," Resa said evenly, eyeing the hostile, unattractive young woman.

"No. He's mine. Mine!" Fanny spat.

Maria came out of the back. Resa looked at her.

"Miss Frazier says she tramples the likes of us in the mud."

In a flash Maria ran behind Fanny. She grabbed the parasol and heaved it across the room. Resa ran out behind the case. One on each side of her, they hustled the kicking, screaming woman toward the door and across the boardwalk. Sir Galahad growled. They pushed her forward, each planting a foot in her posterior.

Miss Frazier screamed.

She landed face down in the mire. A passing wagon weaved around her, covering her with manure-filled muck, splashing her. Sir Galahad stood over her, growling.

She wailed, she screamed, she thrashed.

Maria rushed back inside, brought out the parasol and tossed it on top of the wailing form. Resa pulled Sir Galahad away.

The commotion brought people out to the street.

Crying and screaming, Fanny picked herself up and ran up the street. Sir Galahad followed, nipping at her heels.

Those that missed the incident read about it in the paper the following day.

They were still laughing about Fanny when Jasper helped them move in the next day.

Resa's shell of a house had turned into a showplace. Contrary to fashion, she decorated it in light colors.

"I've seen all the dark evil-smelling halls and red paper I ever want," she whistled through the rooms.

Jasper set down an end table puffing. "It's lovely and so fresh. Just like you."

Resa picked pale blue draperies and ivory wallpaper for the parlor to set off the peach-colored sofa and loveseat which she arranged in front of the white marble fireplace. The Chinese rug on the floor was also pale, with dark blue and orange designs against an ivory background. Some pale blue velvet chairs and marble-topped tables completed the room's decor.

"I've thrown money to the winds," Resa said lightheartedly. "Come see."

The dining room was decorated in pale green throughout except for some Chinese red lacquer boxes that set off the pale green rims of the china in her magnificent china press, which presided over the end of the room in massive splendor. A matching table and chairs, with pale green seats and several ferns on marble pedestals finished the sparsely furnished room. Resa liked the bay windows in the room, the emptiness that showed off the furniture and the large crystal chandelier.

"The people who sold me the furniture thought I was crazy for leaving the walls bare, but I wouldn't change. And," she said, "they're making enough not to argue."

"It's fine," Jasper said with admiration, and fingered the lace sheers at the windows.

The kitchen was pale yellow. Maria took over the room. She brought in plants—geraniums mostly—and put some Mexican pottery she found in a stall on D Street around the shelf that ran up near the ceiling.

"It's not as good as adobe, but it's more like home." Her gap-toothed grin pleased Resa.

Maria hung the canary cage above the plants in a sunshiny window. He was in fine voice. She took the Philpots' rocking chair and put it near the stove. Next to it on a small table, she set her yarn and sewing supplies.

By two o'clock the kitchen was somewhat in order. Chung Ho, the Chinese cook Resa had hired, arrived with groceries. He stacked them on the round oak table and the chairs.

"You and I'll get along just fine, Chung, if you let me run you out now and then so I can make chili and menudo. Like my people eat. But only if I can get the right chilis."

"Yes, miss," Chung replied. He looked puzzled as Maria began to help him put the groceries away in the icebox and in the pantry.

Resa and Jasper carried boxes upstairs to her lavender and white bedroom. Jasper stared longingly at the huge four-poster with its eyelet canopy that dominated her room. She pretended not to notice as she made it up with crisply ironed eyelet sheets.

"Go get the things for Maria's room. They're right by the hall tree."

Into her wardrobe she put only her best gowns, leaving the rest for later.

Resa trudged down the hall to the extra bedroom with a load of baskets and some odds and ends to go to the shop.

"I'm so excited I could dance," she said to Maria, who was making her bed.

"Ugh. I'm so tired, I'm quitting." She looked at the red and white decor, admiring the Mexican blanket that Resa had given her for Christmas. "It looks fine. Let's see if Chung has coffee. I'm too old to do all this at once."

"Tomorrow's another day." They passed Jasper on the stairs, groaning with a final load of Maria's clothes.

"Enough! Let's relax. You've earned a good dinner," Resa laughed at him.

Over dinner, they laughed again about Fanny. Maria disappeared into the kitchen.

"Speaking of the Frazier-Colbert families, I've a favor to ask," Resa said.

"I move you all day," Jasper pretended to complain, "then you still have favors? You'd better hire me."

"Seriously, Jasper," the smile left Resa's lips. "This will help me more than you can imagine. You mentioned land titles in the courthouse. Can you help me find out who owns certain pieces of property here?"

"Colbert? Frazier? Sure. But I'll be in Sacramento until mid-week. I'll get Pierson to take over. We could do it next Friday. But it'll take all day, maybe longer."

Resa squeezed his hand. "Thanks."

"If we find what you're looking for, it'll be the end of us, won't it?" He stirred his coffee.

"We'll always be friends," she said kindly. "I want to ride with you when I get settled again. I love your company."

"Still, you've set your cap for Claude."

"Yes, I won't lie about it. But it may never happen."

Jasper looked woebegone. She patted his shoulder, offered him another piece of pie. He declined.

"All right. I'll do it. But why am I always a day late and a dollar short?" He stretched. "I'd better go. Thanks for a fine day."

"If moving day's fine, I'm a monkey's uncle." She walked him to the door, then got his coat.

"Any day with you is fine." Jasper leaned toward Resa, ready to kiss her. Then, a regretful smile on his face, he drew back, tipped his hat to her, and walked off.

Resa went in, and sat on the sofa in the living room, musing. Maria climbed the stairs to bed. Chung Ho left the kitchen for his quarters behind the house.

Resa was almost ready to go up to bed when there was a banging like a boot kicking at the front door. She cautiously opened it.

It was Claude. In his arms he held the limp, black, panting form of Sir Galahad.

Resa cried out and patted Sir's head.

"He's dying—he's been poisoned. I found him in front of the shop."

"Bring him to the kitchen. Oh, Sir. Please don't die. Please!"

She rushed upstairs and grabbed a blanket. Maria followed her down when Resa called, "It's Sir Galahad. Somebody poisoned him!"

They wrapped him in the blanket by the stove.

"Salt! Maybe we can get him to throw it up." Maria grabbed the salt cellar. Furiously, she pumped water into a pot. "Stoke up the fire. This should be warm!"

As the woman worked, Claude held the dog.

With one last coughing howl, Sir Galahad shuddered, then lay still.

"He's gone. Worst damn dog. Poor damn dog." He brushed at his eyes, then took Sir Galahad's body out the back door.

Resa started to follow.

"Stay," said Maria. "He wants to be alone."

Resa poured whiskey for everyone. She waited for Claude. Maria drained her glass; she made a face.

"I'm going back to bed. Nothing to do now." Maria left.

Resa grew angrier and angrier thinking about Sir. He'd been a pain, a nuisance, but she'd grown to love him. Soon Claude came in.

"I'll take him when I go. It must've been strychnine."

"Who did it?"

Claude took the whiskey and drained it. He held his glass out for a refill.

"I think Fanny. He wouldn't have taken food from a stranger. We had a terrible row two nights ago. The next day you threw her into the mud. She did it for spite."

"That raving bitch," Resa mumbled. She poured herself another drink.

"I'd like to give her poison, make her suffer," she said.

"Oh, she's suffering. She must be at her wit's end," Claude said. "She wants to go to Europe for our honeymoon. She keeps pressuring me about it in spite of the fact that I've told her and told her again that I can't leave now. I'm still needed at the

"Anyhow, the night of the fight we went to a party at Mackays. She announced publicly that she had the tickets and that we are going. You should've seen her. Every old biddy in the place was crowded around her telling her where to go, what to see, what to buy. Oh Resa, when I saw you I knew Fanny couldn't hold a candle to you. But I saw her in her true colors that night. She's greedy. I saw my future—every penny I ever make will go to keeping her in finery and lap dogs.

"After the party, I told her in the carriage that we wouldn't be going to Europe. Sir was with us and he was growling at her. She just kept at it. She called me cheap. She called my father a miser. She stopped then. For a while she blew in my ears, expecting that would change my mind. When it didn't, she yelled and whined like a wounded beast.

"We were in front of her house. Still she kept it up.

"Well, I'd had enough. 'Eyes ahead,' I yelled to my driver. I put her over my knee, pulled up her petticoats and spanked her hard. Sir Galahad nipped her arm while she was trying to hit me back, then he clawed her dress until he ripped it. Her hat fell off and you know how he likes hats.

"She screamed. She hit. I dragged her up the steps and practically threw her in the front door."

"You rotten, terrible man," Resa couldn't suppress her smile.

"I felt awful for about ten seconds after I did it. Anyway, I haven't heard from her since except what I read."

"Is the engagement finished?"

"As far as I'm concerned it is. Rather than marry her, I'll leave. China. Timbuktu. Panama. Anyplace to be away from her."

"Did you propose to your father that you'd find backers to replace Frazier?"

"Yes. He won't hear of it. He talks about breach of promise both to Frazier and Fanny. He talks about honor. He snarls about his lifetime dream. He's even pleaded with me. He and Frazier are best friends. Still, rather than marry her, I'll go.

"I love my family, Resa. I don't want to ruin everything."

"Have you found any backers?" Resa asked.

"The day before the battle, I talked to a man who expressed interest. I need to check his resources."

"Ask your father to come here a week from Monday at seven-thirty. I think I can help. Don't pack for China yet."

"Why do you want to talk to him?" Claude was curious.

She took his glass and set it on the chair. She kissed him. She didn't know what Claude might know about Augustus, but she wouldn't tell him anything.

"Secrets. Trust me. We've had a wild day. You'd better go."

At the threshold she kissed him again, savoring the taste of him. "Don't worry."

"Don't see my father," Claude said protectively. "I tell you, he's a ruthless man, much as I love him. He . . . well, he enjoys power. He uses it. I sometimes think he hides things. Yet I know I'm crazy. He's built his whole career on integrity. He's one've the best people in town."

"I hope you can find a replacement for Frazier. He'll have to give in then."

Hoist yourself on your own petard, didn't you Fanny. You are dumber than I thought, thought Resa sadly to herself as she went upstairs. *I'm sure going to miss that dog.*

Resa and Jasper rummaged through the musty books of land titles the following Friday.

"Sometimes they're not very accurate," Jasper cautioned her. "So many fires in the old days. Sometimes people don't report sales. We'll probably never find what we're hunting."

"Courage," she said as her dirt-smudged fingers turned the pages. Her eyes scanned column after column of entries.

By the end of the day, they had an interesting picture of a firm called C Enterprises. Half the bars and dance halls on B Street rented from it.

"My mind's running wild," said Jasper, as the picture got more and more clear. "If C Enterprises is Colbert, he has plenty to hide. Half the brutality and rape in this town takes place in those dens.

"Colbert's real money is not in the law, it's in all this rotten real estate," Jasper realized.

"Yet, there's still no proof." Resa brushed a few stray strands of hair from her brow with her sleeve.

"Right. If you find it, his congressional race is finished. He'll be excommunicated. Fr. Bernard hates everything to do with vice. He'll be shunned by the mucky-mucks." Jasper chuckled.

Resa left Jasper. She sent a message to Maria that she would be gone all night. At five o'clock, her heart in her throat, she sneaked into a closet in Colbert's office when the secretary's back was turned. She hid until everyone left. Then she opened the door and went directly to Augustus's office.

She rummaged through the office in the last rays of light. There was a safe, but she couldn't open it. There was a set of ledgers, but as far as she could tell, they were all for the law firm. She was stumped. Nothing in the office had anything about C Enterprises. Still, she kept searching.

C'mon. There's got to be something, she mumbled to herself. There were two locked desk drawers but she didn't know how to jimmy them. Still, she persisted. She went through every piece of paper she could find. Nothing. She got to the bottom drawer, after searching through twenty or so around the room. She was frightened, tired, and despairing.

Suddenly, she found what she needed. A rubber stamp with "C Enterprises" on it sat next to a stamp pad. *Yippee!* she breathed. Beneath it was a receipt for a case of Lysol, signed by one Edward Greebe—Big Eddie.

Resa put the grimy stamp in her handbag along with the receipt. She started out the door. Just then she heard footsteps. She opened the door a crack, and in the waiting room stood the scrubwoman. She was mopping, and her back was to Resa. In a moment she'd enter Augustus's office. There was no place to hide. Resa drew her veil over her face, her mind racing.

She charged out the door, directly at the scrubwoman, her hand over her eyes. The woman dropped her mop.

"It's dark. It's dark and I'm ill. The gentleman let me lie on the couch. I fell asleep and he forgot about me. Help me. Let me out! Oh. My head!"

"Thief!" the scrubwoman called. "Thief!"

"No, I'm ill. How dare you call Mrs. Cramer Van Snedden a thief? How dare you!"

Resa waved and bobbed to the scrubwoman, hooking her with determination under the arm. "My head! It's bursting. Let me out!"

The scrubwoman let Resa out the door.

"No affair of mine." She shrugged her shoulders.

"I thought you were going to be out all night," Maria said.

"So did I." Resa panted as she came in the door. "I've just had the damnedest adventure of my life. Get me some brandy," she said to Maria.

Chapter Twenty-One

As Resa poured coffee for Augustus Colbert, sitting on the sofa across the table from her, she was aware that he assessed every hair and curve of her body.

"You're lovely," he said, blowing cigar smoke toward the white ceiling of her parlor.

"Thank you, but it's not my appearance

that's important. I have a favor to ask." Resa paused significantly. "I want you to let Claude out of his engagement to Miss Frazier."

Behind the door, Maria stood, her knife ready. She was praying for Resa, ready to attack.

Augustus laughed derisively. "What business is it of yours?" He sipped his coffee, well-laced with brandy.

"Claude and I are friends."

"Pah," he spat. "You want him, that's all."

"Regardless of my feelings, he detests Fanny."

Again, Augustus laughed. "So, he told you about their fight. His big mouth and your presumptions—kicking her into the gutter—prove you're a snipe. Your 'husband' must have been a fool to teach you such upstart behavior."

"My husband taught me to be watchful."

"And watchful you are. To a fault. Your coffee and brandy have been wasted on me. Claudius Frazier and I will see the union of our families as planned. I'd better be going." He rose.

"I hoped to avoid this," Resa pretended regret. "Now I'm left without a choice." She stood up and faced him squarely, her hands on her hips. "I know about C Enterprises. I haven't told Claude. I'll never tell him, provided you let him drop Fanny and convince Frazier the wedding is off."

"Why you little guttersniping whore." He rose, jostling the table. "I wasn't born yesterday. How dare you make accusations?"

"You don't deny it."

"Deny it? I don't even know what C Enterprises is."

"Don't you?" Resa's heart hammered in her breast. "Twelve blocks of dives and houses all over B Street."

"You're whistling in the dark. Enough!" He glared at her and started out of the room.

"Then why were these in your desk drawer?" She shoved the stamp and receipt into his face. "Your wife and Claude will suffer terribly when the *Enterprise* reports you're the biggest landlord in that cesspool. Think about the church. Fr. Bernard will excommunicate you on the spot."

He was white around his eyes. He raised his heavy arm as if to strike her.

"Hit me. That'll just add more color." Resa withdrew her evidence to keep it safe from Colbert. "Maria."

Maria, knife drawn, came in.

"Take these away," Resa gave her the

stamp and receipt, "then come back." She sat down at the table. "More coffee, Mr. Colbert?

"You needn't bother to send someone looking for the stamp and the receipt. They won't be on the premises if you do. And they won't be in my shop, either."

"Thought of everything, haven't you?" he snarled.

"I'm just protecting you from your dangerous side."

Colbert sat down and was silent for a long time, staring up at the chandelier. Maria came back into the room.

"Put the knife away, Maria. I don't think we'll be needing it now," Resa said.

The grandfather clock in the hallway ticked monotonously. Resa sipped her coffee. She waited. At last he stood. They walked to the entry hall, where Maria, still looking daggers, handed Augustus his coat.

"I do hope Claude finds a backer," she smiled.

"It's not what I'd bargained for, but I guess I do, too," he said heavily as he walked out the door. "Breaking the news to Mrs. Colbert about Fanny won't be easy."

"I'm certain a man of your power will handle it fine."

* * *

277

In the following fortnight, Resa lived in a kind of animated suspension, for she heard nothing from Claude. Since keeping busy was her only salvation, she and Maria cleaned the shop and rearranged the house. She went riding with Jasper Fantana both on Saturdays and Sundays, although it snowed enough to make riding slow. She said very little when they went riding, but practically wore out the chestnut filly borrowed from Fantana, chasing whatever caught her eye. The last Sunday they went riding, they stabled their horses, behind Fantana's house. Resa dismounted and stood, nose pressed to the filly's damp shoulder, while the groom waited impatiently to take the horses. The smell of the stable reminded her of the adobe in the Sangre de Cristos and, as she stood there, she thought of Garcia. She felt his touch. She smelled him. She grew hot in the memory of his kiss, the smoothness of his thighs and neck.

Fantana walked up behind her and caressed her shoulders. Resa turned. She held him. Tears flowed down her face, splotching the wool of his jacket.

"I'll fight him for you," Jasper said, trying to help her, knowing he could not, really.

"It's not that, Jasper. I was just thinking about something that happened a long time ago."

She wiped her eyes and looked tearily up at him. It felt good to be held.

"I hate waiting. I'd rather climb a mountain any day than wait," she said.

"You don't have to wait. I'm here. You know how I feel."

"Let's walk."

At a shop on the corner, Jasper bought her a blown-glass nosegay of violets. Arm in arm they continued down the quiet street.

"I love you, Resa Cluvier. We would be happy," Jasper said.

"Yet it's not possible," she said. "Goodness knows, you'll be one of my best friends all my life. You'll be rich one day. Yet I'm too tired to struggle with you."

"With your pluck you'll never be tired," Jasper smiled down at her.

"I'm tired of worrying about money."

"Rot. If you get it in six months you'll be just as complacent as the other rich folks. Just as high and mighty, just as blue-nosed."

"Sure, I want what you're talking about. But the minute you see me getting wrapped up in things, not doing what should be done, you can push me in the mud like I pushed Fanny."

"And what great things will you do?" he asked.

"I can't tell even you yet. If I do, it'll all vanish."

As fast as it came, her black mood left. She skipped ahead of him, dragging him behind her. "Let's go to the Sharon House for tea. I'm famished."

She and Fantana came up the steps to her house an hour later. Waiting at the entryway was Claude, a bottle of champagne under one arm, a dozen red velvet roses under the other. He looked sternly at them as they mounted the stairs.

"Maria must have gone to the Indians," said Resa, trying to ignore the glances Fantana and Colbert passed between them.

"I've got to be getting back," said Fantana.

"It was nice to ride with you." He waved at her as he ran down the steps.

"Here I've been working like a slave for two weeks to harvest a fat electoral plum and when I come to celebrate, you're out with another man." Resa fumbled with the key and let them in.

"There's something to celebrate?" She was as nervous as if she'd never been alone with a man.

"I'm not standing here with roses and champagne for nothing. It was hard as tying two devils by their tails, but I got my father a backer. Frazier's out. Fanny's out. Resa Cluvier, I love you!" He set the bottle, put the roses on the table and picked Resa up in his arms and twirled her around.

"Hooray! Hooray!" She bent her head down, knocking off his hat. She kissed the top of his head. "You did it! You did it!"

He followed her into the dining room, telling her details. She brushed off her habit, then got champagne glasses down from the china cabinet.

"Let me go up and change. I smell horsey."

"You smell perfumed," he caught her arm. "I don't want to be without you for a second. Find an opener; I want champagne.

She saluted him and bowed. "Yes sir." She vanished into the kitchen.

Claude sat in the parlor, sprawling his long legs out from one of the overstuffed chairs. When Resa came back, bringing the glasses and opener, she studied him.

"You look terrific in that chair. I'd about given up hope of ever seeing you here again."

He opened the bottle and poured the wine.

"Here's to us! To parties without nagging! To a long and happy life together!" He raised his glass.

"Aren't you getting the cart before the horse?" Resa asked, raising one eyebrow.

"Oh, yes." He stood and raised his glass again. "Mrs. Resa Cluvier, will you do me the honor of spending the rest of your life with me?"

"Yes." She raised her glass. They clinked them, and kissed, splashing champagne around them. They set the glasses down.

"I've been so lonely. So very lonely," Resa said. Rubbing his back, she drew him up the stairs.

"Resa, you don't have . . ."

"The nice thing about marrying an orphaned widow is you don't have to care about family and propriety." She lit the lantern in her bedroom, placing it near the window as a signal to Maria.

They undressed each other. He was all thumbs with the row of buttons up her back, but she giggled, tickled him, refusing to let him think, to be serious, to think of her past. Soon she was certain he wasn't thinking about her past anymore.

In long draughts, she slaked her thirst on his body. She touched his toes, his head, his heavily muscled chest. She took him into herself with a joy she thought had died. He was gentle, yet sure of himself. He lay before her like a book with a thousand pages, each of which she wanted to read—again and again.

"I never knew it could be so good." He lay nibbling her ear when they were finished, the covers drawn around them like the luxuriant haze of their bodies. "Fanny'd never let me touch her. The others . . . well," he said, a little abashed, "it's always been a rush."

"And now there's time . . . let's finish that champagne."

"Only if you bring it up here. I just want to lie here and look at you," he said.

She was starting up the stairs with the champagne when Maria burst through the door.

"*Fuego! Fuego! Madre mia!* Fire! *Fuego!* The shop! *Caliente!*"

Resa dropped the champagne. For a second she stared at Maria.

"Go! I'll be right there. Fire wagons?"

"*Pronto!*" Maria ran out. "*Fuego!* Fire. Fire!"

Resa collided with Claude when she rushed upstairs and he down. She threw on her gown and dragged on her shoes and cape. Together they ran through the mud.

Flames jumped high into the sky below them.

By the time they got to the shop, it was an inferno. Flames leapt everywhere—in the bakery, in the Last Chance. Firefighters—men from the bars, off-shift miners—struggled to keep the blaze from eating its way up to C Street, for it had obviously started in The Gilded Cage. The pumper's hoses might as well have been toys. By morning the whole block was gutted, but the fire was a sputtering ghost of its night-long fury.

Resa sat on the boardwalk across the street from the blackened buildings. She was covered with soot and with mud. She sat, while near her, Maria bandaged the forehead of a firefighter who'd been burned by a piece of falling debris. Others, singed and exhausted, milled in the street where a bartender was providing beer. Suddenly Resa started crying, tears dropping from her eyes to her filthy dress.

Claude and Fantana came around the corner. Both were exhausted. They carried picks. Fantana's eyebrows were singed off and Claude's hatbrim was covered with burn holes where sparks had fallen. A third man walked between them, carrying a blackened thing.

"Mrs. Cluvier," he said when Claude had introduced him as Anderson, the fire marshall, "did you keep large quantities of coal oil in your shop?"

"Never. Just a one-gallon can for the lanterns."

"Was this it?" He held out the blackened object.

"No. It's far too large."

"Looks like arson. Who'd want to do this?"

"I've no idea." Resa buried her head in her hands.

"Think about it. If you decide on anyone, let me know. Right now I could use a beer."

"Thanks for trying," she said tiredly.

"Sorry we couldn't do better. Water's such a problem." He strolled off.

Claude and Jasper sat beside her.

"Everything! Gone!" She started crying again. Claude put his arm around her and raised her up.

"Jasper, get us a beer. I need to talk to Claude." Resa turned to Claude and looked deeply into his eyes. She took a breath and said, "It . . . it was your father burned it or had it burned."

Claude gave a start. "Why? In God's name, why?"

"I found out that he owns all the land in

285

the Red Light district. I threatened to expose him if he didn't let you leave Fanny." She started crying again.

"That conniving bastard!" Claude held her.

"I knew he had his fingers in something; I just didn't know what," Resa said between soft sobs.

Jasper brought them beer.

"Fantana, will you rent a horse for me at the livery and meet us at Resa's house in a couple of hours?"

"Sure." Fantana drained his beer. "I'll meet you at nine."

"Don't say anything about who it's for," Claude added.

"Right." He walked away.

"What? . . ."

"He's gone this far, who knows what he'll do? I've a couple men to hire. I'm taking you out of town 'til the excitement dies down. We'll get married in Dayton. Lay low. We've got to leave. I'll kill him if I stay."

"If it wasn't for you, I'd have his name plastered all over the *Territorial Enterprise* by tonight. I can't prove who started the fire, but I've proof about the rest of it."

"I hate him," he shook his head. "God how I hate him."

"The shop wouldn't have been the same

without Sir anyway," Resa said.

They walked up the hill, leaning on one another. The wreckage still smoldered.

"First to the Yellow Jacket. Then my place. Then yours."

"I can go on. Start packing."

"I'm not letting you out of my sight," Claude said fiercely.

When Fantana entered the Lone Star Livery, he noticed a large black and white pinto. He asked to rent him.

"He's not for hire. Belongs to a private party," said the stable hand, chewing on a straw. "Here's a gelding. Will he do?"

Fantana examined the horse. He looked over every animal in the stable and wasn't satisifed with one.

"Can't take a chance. They're all plugs," Jasper said, annoyed.

"It's the best stable in town."

"If so there's plenty people walking when they should've been astride."

"Picky bastard." The hand spat on the floor. Fantana walked out.

He went to his stable and saddled his chestnut. He rode toward Resa's. *Take good care of her . . . Lord, I'm a fool. If only my ship had come in. Hell! She had her mind made up, anyway.*

At Resa's two men stood at the front door. As Fantana dismounted, they drew. One had a .45, the other a .38. The first chewed a cud of candy, the other slouched near the column to the right of the door, his relaxed stance belying his readiness.

Colbert and Resa came out. Both were armed. Resa carried her Sharps. She was pale. Colbert wore a Navy Colt and carried Resa's gear. "He's all right, boys." The men put their weapons back in their holsters.

"Fantana, this is Candy Joe Granger, Harry Weiss." The men nodded to one another.

"You brought your *own* horse?" Claude asked Jasper.

"Nothing decent at the stable. Hell, take him. My wedding present to you. Now or whenever."

"Thanks, Jasper. This sure isn't like I wanted it. We'll celebrate when we get back.

"Thanks, Fantana." Colbert shook his hand.

Fantana shrugged. "Lady's made up her mind . . . take care." He turned quickly and walked away.

"That romantic won't stay unattached for long," Claude smiled. "All right, boys, let's ride, back way down Six Mile. When we get to the top, you double back. Don't leave the place."

They rode through the back streets, north of the city, then doubled back to the north side of Six Mile.

"Take care of Maria," Resa said.

"She looks like she can take care of herself," said Granger. "But we'll keep an eye out." They rode back toward town as Claude and Resa struggled down the canyon, dodging mills and traffic by staying above them.

That night while Maria and Chung Ho were battling Granger and Weiss at poker, Colbert and Resa were married in Dayton. From the bar of the Dayton Hotel, where they were staying, they found two amiable men to stand up for them. "They won't remember much about us in the morning," Resa said.

"I always wanted flowers and a nice wedding," Resa said as they were lying in bed after the ceremony.

"When this blows over, we'll do it right. We'll get married at St. Mary's and have a party." Claude ran his fingers through her hair. "Anyway, I had ulterior motives. I want you all to myself."

"It isn't everybody who gets acquainted after the wedding," she said, then turned to kiss him.

For a week they holed up in Dayton. Yet no one tried anything against them. They saw nothing of Augustus.

"Let's go home tomorrow," Resa said. "I miss the house. Your father's had his pound of flesh."

"When I think about him, I'd still like to kick in his teeth. My poor mother . . . I hope she gives him hell!"

"I hope we can all forgive and forget." Resa was ready to begin her new life.

"Never. Until he personally begs your forgiveness."

"I just hope the house is there when we get back."

"Granger and Weiss will have done fine. They owe me. I've been helping them locate claims for free. We're like brothers. We grew up together and they're tough. Loyal."

Chapter Twenty-Two

On a morning swathed in the ice crystals of pogonip, two weeks after the Colberts returned, Resa and Maria went to the Farley Fish Market. Glued to them, one on each side, were Granger and Weiss. When they got to the market, Granger chewing his ever-present cud of molasses candy, remained at the front door to the shop. Weiss walked in with them, searched the place for any danger, then walked out the back, where he waited in the alley.

"Lord, I'm sick of being followed," said Resa.

"Mr. Claude's right . . . this bass looks good . . . who knows what his father will do? Granger and Weiss know every hoodlum in the city. We need them."

"You'd think Augustus would have his revenge."

"That kind never has enough," Maria said.

"Yeah. Comes trouble, Weiss and Granger'll earn their keep."

They loaded their baskets with crabs and bass. Signalling to Weiss, they left. The men, one on either side, made the women feel uncomfortable.

"We're going to the bakery up the street," Resa said to Granger. "Then home."

"Right. Blasted pogonip. Don't like you out in it."

"It's that or go crazy in the house." She sighed. "I miss The Gilded Cage."

"If this blows over, you'll have another," said Maria.

"Hell, no offense intended, ma'am. If I had all your money, I'd never work another day," said Weiss. "I'd get me a jug of the best bourbon in the country and I'd have me a servant to keep that jug full. I'd dance all night. Sleep all day. Never do nothin' I didn't want." He laughed. The sound was muffled in the fog.

"*Dios mio!* Look!" said Maria.

They were passing a saloon. Looming out of the fog stood a black and white pinto.

Resa jabbed Maria in the ribs. Granger and Weiss drew.

"Never mind, boys. Maria thought she saw a ghost."

"I'm going crazy," Maria said.

"To the bakery," Resa said, trying to sound gay.

"You're sure jittery," said Granger. "Hate to shoot a horse for nothing."

Inside the bakery, Resa ordered two loaves of French bread. "Fool!" she hissed to Maria. "There are a thousand horses like that around."

"I'd know him anywhere," Maria said woodenly.

"Forget it. You want them telling Claude? It's nothing, I tell you."

Still, as they walked home, all four were quiet. By the time they got to the house, the fog was beginning to lift. Candy and Harry stationed themselves, one at the front door and one at the back, hunkering down to their day's watching, playing solitaire with gloved hands. Every hour they came in for a break. Resa kept them supplied with coffee.

Yet the sight of the horse had unnerved her, too. Resa made a nuisance of herself, supervising Chung Ho with the making of deviled crab, until he was annoyed and she was beside herself with the urge to ride out alone for some privacy in the canyons. Maria was knitting. She kept dropping stitches and swearing.

Around two o'clock it started snowing. It snowed and snowed. The snow filled the streets, wrapping them all in tension and soggy discontent. Resa invited Candy and Harry inside.

"They can't torch the place in this," Resa called out the door. "There's no sense you staying out in it."

Maria continued to knit, paying no attention to the clots of snow that came in on the feet of the bodyguards. The Chinese cook hummed a whiny song as he hauled out a kettle and started a broth with the fish bones and heads. Resa read in the parlor for a while, then she went to her room. The snow made her feel boxed in. Nervous. She had had enough of bodyguards, of living in a fortress that was meant to be a home. She tried to get involved in her book, but it was no use. Time hung over her.

Around four o'clock the mail came. She sorted through it after the guards brought it back, swearing at the snow. There was a letter for Claude in his mother's hand. Every day she sent a letter. Every day Claude read it and refused to see her. "I won't go, no matter what, until my father gives in," he said.

At five-thirty Claude came in. Resa kissed him, pouting.

"I hate this. I can't go anywhere without those apes. Now I can't walk outside without getting frozen. I'm so glad you're home."

She poured him a glass of whiskey; she took sherry. They settled themselves in front of the fireplace.

"Was it worth it? This terror and destruction to marry me?" Claude asked her.

She raised her glass to him. "I'd have married you if it started a war. I'm just short on patience. Never had much of it, I guess."

He read his mother's note. "I hate to ignore her. Still, if I know her, it's the only way we'll get my father to be reasonable."

"How so?"

"My mother's quiet. She never says anything about my father's business. She has spent her life caring for him, going to church, taking interest in charities. Yet, she has a will of iron. She'll figure a way." Then he said, "Resa, you'll have to be patient longer. I've got to go to Sacramento next week, to escort a party of investors in from the East."

"Horrible! *Midsummer's Night Dream* is at the opera next Thursday. I want to go."

"If things weren't like they are, you could take Jasper and his new friend, Lily, but we can't chance it."

"It would just be the one evening," she pleaded.

He stroked her hair and brought her head to his shoulder. "There'll be other times."

Maria announced dinner.

Granger and Weiss looked uncomfortable toying with fish instead of the steak and potatoes they were used to. Outside the storm continued. Everyone ate in silence. They were just finishing sand pears baked with honey when the door chime rang.

The guards shot up from the table, guns drawn.

"We'll answer the door," said Granger. Claude rose, motioning Candy and Harry to stay. He went to the hall tree and got his .45 from his holster. Then he went back to the table and stood by Resa. "All right," he motioned. Maria scuttled for the kitchen where her knife rested in her knitting basket.

Augustus, followed by Granger, came into the dining room. Behind Granger, in a tense parade came two strange men followed by Weiss. Augustus's men were armed to the teeth. Everyone held himself by a thread.

Resa leveled her glance at Augustus.

"You call off your jackals, I'll call off mine," said Claude. "Send them in the kitchen."

"Coffee?" Resa said to Augustus, who motioned his men to follow Granger and Weiss.

"No, thank you. I won't be staying long."

"Let's go into the parlor," suggested Resa. Augustus and Claude followed her. Resa couldn't help but be nervous that she couldn't see her father-in-law for the few steps to the parlor. They seated themselves, Resa and Claude on the sofa, Augustus in a chair near the fire.

Augustus lit a cigar and settled himself stiffly into the chair, his poker-faced glance betraying nothing.

"You're a charming couple. Allow me to congratulate you," he said reaching into his coat.

Claude drew his pistol.

"No need," said Augustus, producing a poke. He dropped it onto the marble-topped table to his right. It sounded heavy.

Claude slipped his derringer back in his pocket.

"For the fire?" he said.

"I don't know anything about a fire. Let's just call it a belated wedding gift."

"Thanks, Augustus, what . . ." Resa began, then trailed off.

"Let's just say, Mrs. Colbert—Elise—convinced me. She's never been one to hold a grudge, but she's been hell on wheels these last weeks." He smiled, then rose.

Claude stood. They shook hands. "Your mother told me to ask you for dinner next Sunday," he said. "Hell. Maybe you're better off."

Claude looked at him, silent.

"We'd love to come to dinner," said Resa trying to ease the tension that was growing again.

"I'll bet *you* will," said Augustus. "Call my boys, Resa."

"You're calling off your dogs?" she heard Claude say as she went toward the kitchen.

"For now. But you keep a keen eye on that woman of yours. What she wants, she gets."

Claude laughed.

When Resa entered the kitchen, she broke

up a poker game, in which Maria was cleaning the men. They all wanted a chance to get back at her, but Resa told them in no uncertain terms it was time to leave.

Lord, she thought, *they're as bad as any gang in the city. Wouldn't Fanny Frazier have a fit if she could see my kitchen now.*

". . . threatened to make me sell all my properties and give the money to the church. She even said she'd divorce me and make the courts give her everything. I've no doubt they would have. She's a bear in a fight, your mother."

"Good," said Claude. Both men sounded happier.

Soon Augustus and his bodyguards were gone.

Resa rushed to the marble-topped table and counted the money. "Good Lord, there's ten thousand dollars here. Twice what I had in the shop."

"And every dime hurt him, you can be sure," Claude laughed. "I never saw my father back down before. I admire his courage."

"Courage, pshaw. From what I overheard, it was that or his ruin. Your mother must be something."

"You'll like her, I promise."

"The Lord works in mysterious ways."

She danced around the room. Claude watched her and clapped his hands in time. Candy and Harry cheered her on. Claude poured them all brandys. "Now you can go to the opera. We won't be needing you boys anymore, I hope. But thanks for a fine job." He lifted his glass to the thugs. Resa shouted "Hear, hear."

". . . no more poker," Maria said with regret.

Chapter Twenty-Three

After Claude's departure, Resa indulged herself. She bought a new dress for the opera. It was lavender velvet with violets in tiny clumps caught along the deeply-cut neckline. The skirt, billowing full and elegantly from the V-dipped waist made her feel beautiful. "I wish Claude could see it," she said to Maria.

Lolling on her bed she considered what to do with the money Augustus had paid her for the store, but didn't feel any urgency. *I'm getting complacent just like Jasper said. Still, it won't hurt to think it over awhile. It's delicious to do nothing.* She turned back to her edition of *Leaves of Grass*. It was naughty, spirited, and the best thing, she thought, since Byron.

Wednesday she had her hair done. She had it dyed to black perfection, although when she got home she confessed to Maria that she wished she could grow it back to its original color.

"Are you wearing your peach dress?" Resa asked.

"I'm not going. Granger and Weiss are taking me to the Shay's. Poker's better than your fancy play."

"It's not because of the mess at Doyle's is it? I'll scratch the eyes out of anybody who lifts an eyebrow at you."

"Times change. You're a lady now. You don't need Maria so much."

"Fool. I'll always need you. Just think, someday there'll be babies to look after. I'll always need you, but more than that, I'll always love you."

"You have babies, I stay. Otherwise, I go back to my people. It's too fancy for me here.

I miss my sisters, my cousins."

"Be careful with Granger and Weiss," Resa warned.

"They try anything, I'll give them the treatment."

Resa, Jasper, and his new friend Lily went in Jasper's carriage to the play. Lily was Doyle's oldest daughter. Her red hair gleamed against her white dress. Jasper had invited them and others to his house after the opera for a supper and dancing. Resa was so excited when they walked into the theater, Jasper holding Lily on one arm, her on the other, that she could barely stand still. The opera house was magnificent. It glowed with lanterns of jewel colors. Polished wood staircases twined toward the balcony. People in fancy dress milled about chatting and buying champagne and petits fours. The hall smelled of perfume, cigar smoke and licorice candy. As they started toward their box, Resa couldn't resist touching the heavy velvet paper.

"Easy, Resa. You'll rub a hole in it," Jasper joked.

"I love it so much I could eat it," she said.

"This is your first time here?" asked Lily.

"Yes. But it won't be the last."

"Wait until you see the actors," said Lily. "You'll never want to leave."

They entered the theater and walked toward their box. In front of them stood a crowd of people among whom were Fanny Frazier and a young man, pale as she. She was hanging on his arm.

As Jasper, Lily and Resa moved past the group, Fanny spotted Resa.

"There's the strumpet," she said loudly, "Mrs. Claude Colbert." She marched toward Resa, dragging her escort behind her. "I'll have you know, Resa, I've hired the Pinkertons to dig up everything there is to know about you."

"Can't get enough sour grapes, can you?" Resa answered in a clear voice. "You wallow in whatever mud you find. You're good at it." Resa walked past Fanny. Fantana and Lily followed.

Fanny glared after her.

They seated themselves in their box. In front of them stretched rows of red plush seats. A red velvet curtain covered the stage. On it was a design in gold leaf wrought with flowers and ribbons. A chandelier cascaded from the ceiling in the middle of the room, surrounded by smaller ones over the orchestra pit illuminating the balcony. Resa took in every detail: the cut of that man's coat, the curls of that woman's hair, the festive suspense of musicians tuning their instruments and starting the overture. The house was packed except for an empty box directly across from theirs.

The curtain went up to the audience's applause. On the stage the actors, a company from New York, began their tale of enchantment and love.

Resa was transfixed by the action. She drank in every line, every gesture. At one point, Lily touched Resa's sleeve, whispering "Isn't he wonderful?" Resa, dragged down from the height of her concentration, smiled distractedly. "Fine," she mumbled.

She turned back toward the stage, but something distracted her. She gazed directly across the theater at the box that had been empty. There, an amused smile of recognition on his face, sat Boone Garcia. He was staring at her.

She shivered. Resa drew her shawl around her bare shoulders, wishing it were a cloak of invisibility. *Maybe he's just ogling. Maybe he doesn't recognize me at all.* In vain she tried to keep her hand in repose as it touched her ringlets.

Next to Boone sat Madam Sophie in a gold satin gown with a hat of white ostrich plumes and gold velvet. She nodded as

Boone spoke to her, then glanced at Resa.

Against the scenes on the stage, Resa whirled in her own drama of Badger and Mike dead, of rape and robbery, of Gloria in bed with Boone and the hatred she felt, of the men that had used her. Yet, underlying it all, the love she had once felt for Boone played a chord against the discord.

She turned down Lily and Jasper's offer of a stroll between the acts, saying she was feeling faint.

She sat perfectly still, her head turned to the side so she wouldn't have to look at Garcia.

He can ruin everything I've done. He can give Augustus and Fanny every bit of evidence they need. A plan. God, give me a plan.

Yet, try as she would, she couldn't think things out. The play continued. Her mind whirled. Garcia's eyes never stopped trying to meet hers and several times, she forced herself to look his way.

Ten minutes before what she judged to be the end of the last act, she nudged Lily. "I'm faint. Can we go?"

Jasper held her arm firmly. Lily walked ahead of them. Resa tottered against Jasper, hoping he'd buy her story.

"Deuced luck," he said as they rode along

in the carriage. Resa sat by the open window, gulping air.

Lily helped her up the stairs and into her bed.

"Do you want me to stay with you?"

"No. Maria will be home soon. My stays must have been too tight, that's all."

As soon as Lily left, Resa jumped from her bed. She paced, wearing a trail in the rug. Still her thoughts were a blur.

"Come in for a while. Have a drink." Maria had come home and Resa heard her invite her friends in. They were laughing.

"I'm sorry, Maria. I came home ill." She turned to Weiss and Granger. "Another time." She escorted them to the door. She was shaking. "I need Maria. Something's come up."

"Anything we can do?" Granger asked.

"I don't think so, but I'll be in touch if I need you. Next time you play poker, you'll have your cup of cheer."

Resa told Maria about her night at the opera. Lights burned in the house until after midnight while they planned strategies for every threat Garcia might pose.

"You'll have to do it alone," said Maria as they walked up to bed. "If he knows I'm

307

here, he'll be extra careful."

"I know. I'll do it."

"He'll never get caught a second time," Maria stated.

"That depends on what he wants and how he plans to get it."

They went to bed; but neither woman got any sleep.

Chapter Twenty-Four

In the early afternoon, there was a knock at Resa's door. She motioned to Maria; Maria vanished upstairs.

Resa opened the door. Boone's black frock coat made him more handsome than Resa remembered. In her apprehension, she hadn't thought of him as a person. Until that moment he had been a cruel memory, an evil force. Presented with his reality, his sexuality, a surge of warmth and chills ran through her.

"Hello, Resa. Or is it still Resa?"

"Boone. Come in. Quickly."

He laughed. "Afraid your neighbors will gossip?"

"What do you want?" She stood with her back to him, vainly attempting to compose herself. Firewhistles and sirens went off in her head. *Fight it! Hold on!*

"You've something that's mine. I've come to collect."

"Let's go someplace. Not in my home."

"Fine. I've rented a brogham."

"I won't be long." Her voice sounded to her as though it were drifting out of a rotted log. "Make yourself comfortable."

Upstairs, she changed into the most proper dress she could find. Maria came in motioning for her to be careful. Soundlessly, she handed Resa her derringer. Resa strapped it to her leg. As she started out, Maria raised her eyes to heaven and made the sign of prayer with her hands.

"Buttoned yourself right up to the eyebrows, didn't you?" Boone remarked as he held the coat she took from the hall-tree. "Such a lady."

"Just a moment. I've got to leave a note

310

for my husband," she said as she went into the parlor. She scrawled a message on her stationery at the desk. They went down the stairs in silence and entered the coach.

"Any scenic ride will do," Boone barked to the driver.

"You've been a busy little girl since I saw you last," Boone said, charm and sarcasm mixing in his voice. "Husband. Fine house. The least you could say is 'thanks.'"

"You left me no choice. I've the money to pay you back and I will. With interest."

"That'll do for a start, but it's not all I want."

"What, then?" she asked.

"I want you and Maria to come south with me. I've quit gambling. That is, I gamble on land now. No more poker. I sold the house in Santa Fe."

"Maria's not with me," she lied. "Couldn't take city life. I sent her back to Santa Fe." She looked out the window. She knew her duty. She knew what she wanted, Boone was holding her hand. What Resa wanted battled with what she felt.

"Have you been here long?" she asked.

"About six weeks. I'll be leaving in two days."

"If I hadn't gone last night . . ."

"I'd have missed you. Had a devil of a

time looking for you. How did you vanish from Santa Fe, anyhow?"

"My secret."

"At least Sophie could tell me about you. It saved me time."

"So *that's* Madam Sophie," Resa faked her innocence. "I've read about her house."

"I'll bet you have. She told me about the recent scandal in the Colbert family. You didn't have anything to do with it, did you?"

"What? Of course not . . ." The pressure of his hand was almost more than she could bear. Suddenly she laughed, removed her gloves. "I must confess, it's good to see you."

"You're suffering from stuffiness but, it's what you've always wanted." His eyes twinkled. "Money. Power. Still, it's no good without a man, is it?"

"I have a man. Claude's a wonderful person. All the things you're not: kind, generous and he loves me."

"And you? How do you feel?" He ran his fingers along the collar of her coat and stroked her neck. He started removing pins from her ringlets.

"Stop it! You've no right," she feebly pushed him away.

"Of course I've the right. I'm your long

lost husband returned from the dead. Sophie told me that story, too. God, I love your
hair black."

She jerked her hand out of his and busily
tried to put her hair back in place. She was a
bowl of Chinese noodles.

"I thought we were going to talk business," Resa said, shaking. "If we can't, stop
the carriage. I'll walk back."

He smiled. "This is business. Your
business, or have you forgotten? You did it.
I didn't make you walk down those stairs.
You did it all by yourself. And you enjoyed
it. Admit it, Resa."

"I didn't enjoy you selling my mother's
jewels. I hated being a whore. *I hated it!*"

"Gloria was an afternoon's diversion. But
you were so damn moral. Moral like only a
kid can be. You were impatient. If I'd
wanted to make a whore of you, I'd have
turned you out when I opened the house. I
wanted to keep you away from the life. You
insisted on it. You!"

"And you never lifted a finger to stop
me," she retorted.

"Would you have let me? Would you have
believed me? You and your all-fired high
horse. You?"

"You might have tried . . ." she was
crying. She was wedged up against the

313

corner of the carriage, as far away from his words as she could get. She sobbed. Her body wracked with the truth of what he said. It seemed to her that all her life she'd been running from herself, putting a respectable hoist house over a shaft full of muck.

Boone patted her hand. She sobbed even harder. He gathered her to him. She was a rag doll, clinging to his chest. At last she reached in her purse and brought out a handkerchief. She dried her eyes and moved back to the corner of the coach.

"All I've wanted was to live respectably, to live well. I've prayed only to have peace, that God would help me be decent."

"Well, the Lord helps those, and you've certainly helped yourself."

They rode in silence. They were passing the cemetery. Momentarily, Resa reflected how lovely it would be to climb into one of the graves.

"Don't look so gloomy, love. You'll see. With me, you'll be happy. At least you won't have to be somebody you're not."

"But I am what you think I'm not. Can't you understand? I'm Mrs. Claude Colbert. I like it. The little girl, the trollop, they're dead. I killed them."

He reached over and pulled the curtains on the coach. "If you can say you've killed

314

what we have, I'll curse you forever for a liar." With abandon, he unpinned her hat and threw it into the corner. She gave in and kissed Boone with a lust that drained her good intentions. She untied his tie. As he kissed her neck, he unpinned her ringlets, scattering the pins everywhere over the velvet cushions, the folds of her skirt. She helped him out of his coat; he struggled with the row of buttons down the front of her dress.

"Damn. You ladies and your fences," he whispered.

"You love every button of it, and you know it."

She removed his shirt. In the muted light of the coach, she studied his bare chest. She ran her fingers over his muscles, her closed eyes memorizing his contours like a blind man memorizing a face. Meanwhile, he stripped her of her corset. "It's like assaulting a fort," he said as he bent toward her, caressing her.

Soon they were both lying amid the plunder of their clothes. He laughed when he discovered the holster with the derringer. "Always prepared." He unfastened it and tossed it in the corner with her hat.

"Lie back. I just want to look at you. You were never so fine as you are now. I'd kill for you. God in heaven, I've never loved anyone but you; I never will."

Resa looked at him, memorizing his lithe darkness reddened with the glow of the sunlight behind the curtains. They stared at one another, transfixed with their heat, with the warmth of the sun, with the swaying of the coach, with velvet and crinoline and cotton. They were drunk with need.

"You're killing me," she whispered. She grabbed his hand and kissed it. She licked his fingers, slowly.

There was a hint of a victorious smile playing around Boone's lips as he looked upon Resa's rapture. But it soon vanished as he succumbed to her artistry.

At first, Resa stroked him gently, like a Muse delicately playing a lute. She feared that Boone would disappear, and for the flash of a moment, she thought he might be playing a trick on her, enticing her only to humiliate her.

But the spark of panic died before it could ever burn into a flame. Instead, love's flames ignited within her, and soon Resa and Boone were gripping each other in a tight embrace.

As Boone traced a trail of kisses down her neck and to her breasts, Resa's hands sought his soft black curls that had always enchanted her. He still smelled of cedar and sweat, and his scent intoxicated her until she felt she was the girl who had lain with Boone under the stars on the vast plain.

He leaned her back on the cushions of the seat of the brogham. As Boone tongued first one erect nipple, then the next, Resa arched up to him, impatient to be one with him again, eager to lose herself in the oblivion of passion she felt only with Boone.

As the setting sun bathed them in its dying rays, it lit their glistening bodies. They glowed with love.

Resa screamed as she clawed red tracks into his back, branding him with her release.

"Damn cat." His passion made her wish she could never let go. He raised himself up against the cushions and they lay in a dream, united in passion and parting, in love and in hate.

"End of the line unless you want to go to Reno," the driver called.

They both laughed. She raised her eyebrow at him. "You really want to go down the Geiger?" she said, her voice full of honey.

"To hell with it," he called. "Take the long way back."

They enjoyed the ride and each other. Later, she loved him again, drove him to a fury before the coach approached town.

"I lied to you this afternoon," she said, as she put on her clothes, giggling as she separated his from hers. "Claude's in Sacramento. He'll be there until Friday. We can spend these days together."

"And then?"

"You'll go back to the south, I'll stay here. Too much has happened for it to be otherwise."

"But . . ."

"Come late tomorrow afternoon. I'll pay you then," Resa said, matter-of-factly.

"You're not going with me?" he asked, surprised.

"What we have is memories. Memories and the physical. What I have with Claude isn't so risqué," she admitted, "but it's what I want."

"Think about it," he urged her. "We could be two days gone before he comes back. We could lose him."

"I don't think I'll change my mind."

She saw herself to her door as the coach pulled away. She knew what she must do.

Chapter Twenty-Five

In the red-gold dawn of the next day, Maria left the house. She walked purposefully down the hills, into the hell of B Street. Her blank expression concealed the tension of her body, against which pressed an arsenal—a knife and a derringer. She felt uncomfortable. She mumbled about craziness.

She seemed to pay no attention to the early morning hangers-on, yet she was coiled to spring.

Into the putrid alleys she charged, her vitality contrasting with the laconic shuffle of alcoholics in doorways, of dogs asleep in the streets, of pigtailed Chinese opening their shops, of cats stretching awake, of thugs draped over the tables of bars, whose open doors let in the weak alley shade.

She noticed every nook and cranny of the neighborhood. When she was satisfied, she strode down the hill to the Indian camp.

In her bedroom, Resa stood before the mirror. She combed her hair back, surveying her face. Dark circles under her eyes made her grab for powder, which she hadn't used since her days in Santa Fe. She rested her head in her hands for a moment before she took her brush and stroked her hair with vigor, as though she'd gladly pull every strand from her head. *Now it's done. Yet what if he changes his mind? Now it's done. Why? Why? God damn you, Boone Garcia, why?* As she jabbed pins into her hair, fashioning it into her customary tight chignon at the base of her neck, she poked her hand. "Hell!" She threw herself on the bed and pounded its snow-white coverlet. She lay quietly, face down. When she arose, she took up her pins again, this time putting them in more gently.

When she was finished, she stared into the mirror. She stood, making certain every hair was in place, every grain of dust removed from her black skirt, her plain shirtwaist shiny white. Quickly she pinned on the amethyst brooch. She pricked her finger, then licked away the blood. A wry smile greeted her in the mirror. "Even when you're not here, you hurt me," she said. Yet she pushed back her shoulders and sucked in her stomach as she resolutely left the room.

"You'd better take the day off, Chung Ho," she said to the cook. "Maria and I won't be home." He bowed.

At the Wells Fargo, she ignored the questioning look of a new teller, who was obviously surprised that a slip of a girl had thirteen thousand dollars to withdraw. After filling the carpetbag she had brought with her, he carried it out to her waiting carriage.

Back at the house, she counted the money into bright stacks of five hundred each. They glowed against the dark wood of her desk. Then she took fifteen hundred dollars and hid them upstairs in her wardrobe. She removed a large handbag, put a floppy white cap into it that she'd made the night before. She went to the kitchen and took a stiffly starched white apron out of a drawer. Folding it, she put it in the handbag. Then she went into the parlor and put the bag down next to the desk. She paced. She paced, staring at the ceiling. The clock in the hallway drove time into her. It was three o'clock. She walked in time with the ticking, her eyes shut against the sunlight which flooded the room.

When the knocker hit its brass plate at the front door, she was startled. She smoothed her skirts as she walked to the entrance. Her hands were shaking. She shook them and forced herself to relax.

They embraced in the hallway.

"I've got your money." They entered the parlor.

He chucked her under the chin.

"I figured the interest. Came up with ten thousand two-fifty bills." She pointed to the piles of money on the desk.

He seated himself and counted it. "Not that I don't trust you."

"I've a valise for it."

"Thanks, I've one in the coach. Didn't want to appear too eager."

"Liar," she said rubbing his shoulder.

"Shall I send the driver away or tell him to wait?"

"Let's go out."

She watched him bound down the stairs. Her heart pounded in her chest. The way he counted the money, she knew she was right. Soon he'd tire of her again.

"Are you coming with me?" he said as he loaded the coins.

"Forever or for the afternoon?"

"Don't be coy," he smiled into her eyes. "Forever."

"No. Let's take what we can from the next two days. It's more than most people ever get."

"I won't take 'no' for an answer," he said determinedly. "You mean too much to me. Besides, you'll love Los Angeles. It's ready to bust wide open; it's not settled like this."

"It's a hog wallow. I've had enough hog wallows."

"I'll make you rich, Resa," he said softly. "Richer than Croesus." He held her, and started playing with the buttons on her shirt.

"You're really serious about real estate? About not gambling anymore?"

"Of course. I only want the good life with you, although I may indulge in some friendly poker now and then. You'll see, I've changed." He sounded sincere.

"But I've all the money I need now. Why should I throw it away for your wild scheming?" she challenged him.

"Because, my soiled dove, it you don't, I'll have to tell Madam Sophie about you. She'll relish getting back at Augustus Colbert with the news."

"I'll bet." Resa's voice did not betray her fear.

"She hates Colbert and she'll ruin you with glee. What will the news do to your dear Claude?"

He tilted her chin up and looked in her eyes. "Tell me that you won't be miserable without me. You'd never have given in yesterday if you didn't feel anything."

Resa wrenched herself out of his grasp and walked toward the window. She closed her eyes and plunged into the future.

"All right. I can't stand to hurt Claude, I'd rather he be pitied for marrying a faithless woman than for marrying a whore. But give me time. For God's sake, give me time. I could join you in a few weeks. I'll break it to him gently."

"Let him come home and find a note. It's easier. Besides, in a couple of weeks, you could be in Hong Kong or Chicago. You have until tomorrow."

"You're sure handy with pressure."

"You're a filly who needs a strong hand. That's your attraction, damnit. I promise you'll never regret it."

She came to him, her eyes wide. "You never promised me anything." She held him, kissing his chin. "I want to celebrate. You want to hear a secret? Ever since I've been in town, I've wanted to go to a dog fight. There's one tonight at the Bull Run, on B Street. Let's go. I'll pack tomorrow. We can leave early Friday."

"Your curiosity amazes me. A girl can get had down there," he said, massaging her back, pressing her closer to him.

"I wouldn't be had if I went with you."

"All right. We'll drop the money at my hotel on the way."

"I was certain I could talk you into it. So I got a maid's hat and an apron. Keep us from getting robbed." She laughed. "I feel so wicked."

"Maybe just for old time's sake, I'll bet on the hounds," he said, his eyes glinting at the thought.

"It better be the last time or, so help me God, I'll leave you."

"I promise."

"That's two."

They went into his hotel, the Stanyon, on south C Street. He left the money in the vault. Resa noticed he put the receipt in his upper right coat pocket. In five minutes of good-natured wrestling with him, as the coach made its way up C Street, she'd relieved him of the receipt. Pretending a coughing fit, she reached into her handbag to get a handkerchief and dropped the paper into it.

"Let the coach go. We'll catch a hack later." She smoothed the rumples from her dress and donned her maid's cap and apron. "There. Don't I make a fetching scullery maid?"

"Whatever you want," he smiled, bowing to her. She climbed from the coach. The passersby saw a tall man, dressed like a gambler escorting a fair-but-frail into the Red Light District. One fat woman, in a lavender hat, raised her nose and sniffed as she passed them.

Arm in arm, as they strolled away, Resa and Boone were laughing. "Now those are the kind you need your derringer for." He patted her leg.

They gagged down salty salami, cheese and slabs of sourdough bread with mustard that passed for the free lunch at Canterbury

Hall. The beer Resa drank tasted green, but she needed its effect.

"This here's Rita," said Boone, introducing her to nobody in particular. "After tomorrow you can find her at the Dew Drop Inn." He winked at Resa. "Yes sir, I like to introduce my girls around 'fore they start."

"Why not now, mister," said a miner next to Resa. He reached for her.

She glared at him.

"I said tomorrow," said Boone. "Lady's new in town."

"Two dollars says she starts now."

Boone quietly drew his pistol and shoved it into the miner's face.

"And I say tomorrow. 'Sides, she's a five-dollar girl."

"Give it to him, Shorty," somebody called.

"Nah. For five bucks I can have ten down at Sophie's."

"Stop the advertisements," said Resa, her teeth clenched. "I said I want to see the place, not get killed here."

Boone laughed. "You mean you're not ready to go back to work?"

"It's no joke, Boone."

They strolled up the street looking in clothing stores. In front of one a stringy old woman with a thick Jewish accent hawked flannel shirts that were stacked in confusion on tables.

"Buy yourself a nice shirt here. Buy your son a nice shirt here," she called. Resa went through the shirts. They were worn almost through. One was like Peter's, the one she'd worn after Boone saved her. She drew it to her cheek, holding it tightly with her eyes closed. Then she dropped it back on the table. They walked away.

"You touch, you buy. You touch, you buy," chanted the woman. Then, "Buy yourself a nice shirt here; buy your son a nice shirt here."

Two doors up was a junk shop. They went in. Inside was chaos. From the ceiling hung ancient, worn harnesses and tack. Reins drooped from bridles toward the mountains of junk on the tables—flat irons; dented pots and pans; worn shoes, smelling of glue; stacks of cheap fabric, its sizing stinking; glass vases; glasses; cups of tin; plates with Chinese writing on them; and broken toys. Mingling with the musty odors, attempting to drown them, was the odor of cooked cabbage. A row of bottles, filled with various home remedies, stood in front of an ancient man with glasses, whose palsied hands reached out to them. "If you want it, it's here," he said. And when they turned to leave, he spat after them, the stream of his tobacco spit missing Boone by an inch, splattered on some fly-specked China instead.

"That salami made me dry. Let's get to the fight. I need a beer," Boone said.

As they pushed their way through the crowd at the Bull Run, groping for a beer, Resa wished she didn't have to stay.

On the stairway from the cellar to the main floor, crowds were gathered—girls from the Bull Run, girls from other houses, and men of all stripes and nationalities. A large coterie of Chinese stood near the ring, which was draped with soiled bunting. On the stairs up to the stalls above, on the floors, standing on the bar, on tables, and on chairs, a mass of motley humanity cheered.

The first of three advertised fights had been held. A Chinese trainer hauled a dead pit bull from the ring, while the victorious handler dragged his snapping, drooling dog—blood staining its coat near its shoulder and splattered all over its chest—around the ring as people tossed money in.

A little while. Only a little while. Resa pulled her hat down.

People were collecting on their bets. Beer flowed as the bar girls circulated through the crowd with pitchers, barely able to keep up with the demand. Somebody spilled a drink down Resa's dress.

They pushed their way near the ring. Boone handed Resa a beer. "You wanted excitement," he yelled, "you got it."

She was buried in the crush of men around her, she could see little except buttons on shirts and jackets. Her cap sat on her head at a crazy angle. She struggled for some room to set it straight.

The crowd roared. "Make way," somebody yelled. The victorious dog and his manager retired; into the ring came two more managers with two more growling, dogs. The dogs were muzzled, straining against their leashes, growling and snapping against the restraints.

The din slacked a little. Expectancy electrified the room as the managers first removed the leashes and collars—holding their beasts with hands in heavy leather gloves. Then, they removed the muzzles. The dogs strained at one another. The killer instinct flexed their muscles and set their massive jaws.

For effect, the men held the straining dogs. "Go! Go!" The crowd screamed in unison.

When the excitement was at a fever pitch,

the men let go and leaped out of the ring.

The dogs were on one another instantly, each striving for the other's jugular. They rolled around the ring in fury, each seeking the other's throat while trying to avoid the jaws of steel with teeth like rapiers. They scratched. They lunged. One, a brindle, tore at the other's face. Blood spurted into the air. Resa's hat was covered with it. She looked at the gray dog who was bitten. One eye dangled from its socket. Yet no one made an attempt to stop the carnage, as the attacker, sensing victory, instantaneously changed its grip and sunk its teeth into the throat of its disoriented opponent. Yet the weaker one tried again. As blood was spurting from its wound, it shook loose and sunk its teeth into the brindle until, its strength ebbing, its knees buckled and the brindle bull stood heaving over its victim, who quivered in death on the plank floor.

"I won! I won!" Boone said. He collected his bets. "All right, ladies and gentlemen, place your bets for the next fight with me," he called. "I'm taking on all comers."

"Boone," she called. "I've got to go out back." He nodded. "I'm taking on everybody," he yelled.

As she elbowed her way through the crowd, she put up with the groping touches that the men gave her. *Only a little while. Only a little while.* She turned when she got to the door. She could see only his arm, raised above the crush, holding two coins. Her head was reeling from the noise, from the blood, from the sweat and smoke. She stumbled through the door, seeking relief in darkness, in the putrid outhouses in the alley.

She took her time. When she came back into the alley, she could hear the crowd screaming with the next fight.

She rushed to the Bull Run's front door. She opened it and stepped inside. She listened. She watched Boone's hand waving above the crowd, full of money. Suddenly his hand dropped. His head vanished.

"Murder!" A woman's voice screamed. "Help! A man's been murdered!"

Maria came out of the crowd to the front door. Together she and Resa quickly walked down the dark street. As they walked, Resa dropped the bloodsoaked maid's cap in an alley. Reaching in her handbag, she fetched out a small dark pillbox with a heavy veil, which she tied over her face. Then she dropped the limp apron into a trash box on the corner. Maria dropped her bloody shawl there too.

You've done it, Maria. You've done it.

The words coursed through Resa's mind. At C Street she hailed a hack.

"The Stanyon Hotel," she told the driver.

Just a little while. Just a little while. Maria asked the driver of the hack to wait. She remained. In the Stanyon, Resa accosted the night clerk.

"Help me! My husband's been run down. They've taken him to the hospital. I need our money. Hurry!"

The clerk looked sleepily at her.

"You have a receipt?"

"Of course. Here."

He looked at her and shrugged. He went into the back room and came out with the money. He signalled to the bellboy, who helped her carry it to the hack.

"Damnfool woman," he said to the bellboy when he returned. "She'll like as not get robbed carrying it out at night."

"They're dumb, all right," said the bellboy. "Beats me why she needs it if he's in the hospital."

"Who knows what goes on in the mind of a woman," said the clerk, picking up the apple he had been chewing.

At Resa's house there was no rejoicing, just a young dark woman crying into her bath water, as an older dark woman sponged her off, patting her on her heaving shoulders.

"It's over."

"School's out," said Resa, wiping her eyes with a bubble-covered hand.

"Claude'll be back tomorrow. What you going to do then?"

Resa looked up at Maria. Without a pause, she said, "I'm going to found a dynasty."